Through These Wicked Nights

Book Two: The Guardians of the Night

Pixie Lynn Whitfield

© Pixie Lynn Whitfield 2013

Credits and permissions:
Cover model—Lynn West; Photographer—Julia Starr Night Fate Photography

Cover Design:
Taylor Jenkins and Pixie Lynn Whitfield

Other works by Pixie Lynn Whitfield:

Darkness Comes This Way
The Night Unleashed: A Short Story Collection

∴

Prologue

"We can't allow these vile creatures to live among us! They drink blood! They'll murder us, our children, control and enslave us!"

Static.

"How long have they been a part of our world? What made these freaks? Scientists want to know..."

Click.

"As the President I can assure you, we are making great strides in working with other countries and military. We will bring them all down before they end the human race. Now is the time for peace among humans. We must work together, trust each other. Do not take matters into your own hands, because we don't want mass panics or wrong decision-making. If you see what you think may be a

Vampire, call the number on your screen immediately and make a report."

Static.

"We will find them and we will kill them."

****

Zarah Duncan walked silently through the Hiders' manor, looking around in horror. They were all dead. She had been too late. An emergency call from one of the Guardians' contacts had come through about an hour before, and as her and the team packed up to head over to the manor for assistance, the Hiders there had all been brutally slaughtered.

The problem weren't Rogues anymore. Even they, the small amount left in the region anyway, were scarce, keeping a low profile.

No, the problems now were humans.

"Zarah!"

"I'm in here!" she called in response. She heard footsteps padding heavily through the doorway, crunching over broken glass and debris. When she turned, her partner Draven Kinsley, stood nearby staring in shock at the gruesome scene around them.

"What happened here?" he breathed, quickly covering his mouth and nose with his free hand, while the other still gripped a gun.

"Humans. A raid."

Zarah looked around at the destruction. The bodies, what was left of them, had been left about with all of the manor's shades and windows open for the sunlight to catch and turn to ash in the morning rays. Bullet holes and blood were splayed upon the walls and drapes. One Hider's decapitated head sat at the body's feet. A once beautiful oriental rug was now a stained mess of mud and blood, and broken glass and shredded books littered the floors. It was a small family, and they had all been gathered in the main room when the unsuspecting raid struck, the television still blaring as it flared with static every so often. Her eyes landed on the child across the room and rage seethed through her. The girl probably had been no more than eight years old, half-human and not fledged yet, but there she lay in her final resting place among her parents and a few other relatives. The beady black eyes of the doll she had been clutching seemed to be staring right at Zarah.

With a raging scream, Zarah balled up a fist and turned to throw it into a nearby wall.

"We were too late!"

One

Zarah had to be dragged out of the manor while she continued to seethe with rage. Draven struggled to keep his hand around her wrist as she resisted his grip, screaming murderous curses. Her brother, Thomas, waited at a sport utility vehicle along with two other Guardians, Markus and Jerry. The night air was crisp and clear, with the cold, late autumn settling in, but the weather didn't affect any of them.

"What the hell happened?" Thomas asked, frowning. He stepped forward and looked at his sister.

"We were too late. There's nothing else we can do here."

Her fangs flashed as she hissed and wrestled her arm away from Draven finally. He continued to watch her warily. Ever since her change a few months ago, she was a constant rollercoaster while her emotions still continued to try and find a solid balance. Zarah always feared she wouldn't find that perfect balance. After all, she had the Elemental Power and both Fallen and Vampire through her bloodline. It was such an unusual mix and maybe it was all making her a little crazy. The growing situation with the humans wasn't helping matters with her volatile emotions either.

"What do you mean? The Hiders..."

"They're dead. Raided. Let's go. The manor has been left with the shutters open for the sun to take care of the bodies. I don't want to go back in there again." Zarah cut her brother off and headed toward the vehicle. She put her gun back in its holster on her hip and pushed past Draven without another word. The men exchanged uneasy looks before climbing in behind her as they headed back to The Compound.

The Fallen were waiting for them in the lobby when they returned. It was obvious they wanted a report of everything that had happened, but she was in no mood to deal with Seth or his group. Instead, she kept walking past in silence without a glance or acknowledgement.

"Something go wrong out there?" Seth asked with a frown. She almost snorted in disbelief at his show of emotion.

It seemed the more time the Fallen spent with them, the more they learned to channel what it felt to be human. Mainly because not long ago, Zarah told them all to quit being emotionless creatures and learn what life was like. It didn't really work too well, but it seemed that through some time and effort, some were trying. Namely Seth.

She continued to ignore them and their quizzical looks as she kept walking onto her room.

"Wait, Zarah—"

Draven caught up to her. Her stomach knotted when he approached. Things had been strange between the two of them over the last several months, but her feelings for him hadn't changed. She turned around and let out a frustrated huff, freezing when meeting his striking blue-silver eyes. Even before his change, his gaze had mesmerized her at times. Now he simply froze her in place with a single glance. She swallowed before forcing her eyes away from his and crossing her arms over her chest.

"What do you want, Draven?"

"I want to talk. Not just about tonight, but about other things. What has been up with you lately?"

She shook her head in annoyance and rolled her eyes. When she reached for her room's door handle she said, "There's nothing to talk about really."

She knew she had been withdrawing from him again like before. As she closed her door in his face and headed toward the shower, shedding clothes along the way, tears stung at her eyes.

The hot water running over her head and back relaxed her, soothing her tense muscles and easing her racing mind of the night's events. It had been four months since Vampires had been made public, and the world was thrown into chaos. Humans were driven by terror and misunderstanding of the species, immediately set on killing all of them. Of course, the Guardians had always known this would happen because humans just didn't always take the time to understand things. She hadn't been alive during the Civil Rights' movement, but her father had and she remembered him telling her about it when she was little before she'd been fledged. Yes, humans came around to finally making peace mostly amongst each other, granting equal rights among all, but she couldn't hold high hopes that Vampires would get the same outcome this time a hundred years later. Providing enough lived through all the chaos to even see a possibility of equal rights and peace with humans.

 With a streak of her hand, Zarah wiped the steam away from the mirror after she stepped out of the shower and stared at her reflection. Her innocent, young appearance stared back. She had only been nineteen when Thomas turned her fully into Vampire. Or "fledging" to make the official term when it came to changing a half vampire-born being into a full vamp. Long, dark auburn waves fell down her back as she dried her hair and it framed her forever-young round face. Her eyes were big with an unusual swirling mixture of amethyst and turquoise. It was part of a trait that she had only just learned about a few months ago; she was half Fallen.

She wasn't tall, only a couple of inches over five feet, lean and athletic. Despite her young or fragile-like doll appearance, the other Guardians knew not to cross her.

After getting ready for bed, she grabbed a book from her overflowing bookshelf and lay down to relax. Her mind was too distracted for reading though, and kept racing with thoughts of the Hiders back at that manor and the untimely end they had met. The doll's beady eyes continued haunting her. Images of large, black pools filled with agonizing screams and blood splatter flashed into her mind. Sighing, she set her book aside and banged the back of her head into the wall behind the bed out of frustration.

Zarah stared up at the ceiling for a long time without moving until one of her fingers twitched involuntarily. She could feel the power in her, still pent up from earlier. Looking down at her open palm beside her, she lifted it and concentrated. Within seconds, a violet floating flame erupted in the center of her hand. She began playing with it by bouncing her hand, causing the flame to jump along in unison.

The anger slowly started to melt away as Zarah's energy leveled and a small smile tugged at her lips. Her elemental powers from the Fallen side had grown considerably over the last few months. It was a magical hum that called to her. Desire that raged from somewhere within her heart for it. A power she'd never be able to ignore, even if she tried.

A knock at her door interrupted her, but the flame didn't go away. She looked up briefly enough to call out a "Come in," and then returned back to staring at her hand.

"I knew I was sensing some elemental use going on," Seth said from her doorway.

Zarah's flame extinguished with a whoosh then and she sighed. Glancing across the room, she met the Fallen's gold irises and forced a tight, polite smile. He was tall, almost touching the top of the doorframe.

"Now what do you want, Seth?" Her voice was rigid. The question may have sounded rude, but she didn't care.

Sometimes, the Fallen made her uncomfortable. Especially him. Of course, Zarah wouldn't admit that out loud.

"I haven't talked to you much since the party."

Zarah nodded. She remembered what he was talking about. The night after they all gathered at their new Compound building when the old one had been destroyed by Rogues, they'd had a party to celebrate despite the coming problems. Nathanial Bolt, her old boss over the Guardians had gone corrupt starting the entire mess that led to the insane world now. He had taken blood samples from Thomas, knowing that she and her brother came from a Fallen mother, and made Rogues intelligent, then arranged an ambush that led her brother to being turned Rogue, which in turn made Thomas turn her Rogue because he knew the family secret that she would cure. Her old mentor tried to kill her for the sake of power and gain in the end and it ensued in a fight at an old military base that made Vampires public. She killed Nathanial but not proudly. His betrayal still stung.

Turning her attention back to Seth, she shrugged.

"I haven't had reason to talk."

In truth, she was confused. He'd kissed her cheek at the party while playing around, and something had stirred. She loved Draven, wanted to be with him, but things were strange between them at the moment. Sometimes he acted like all he wanted was her, and then other times he was cold and distant like old times. It was like a battle. And it was one that she was not going to fight. She was not the type to chase after any guy. If he wanted her, he'll tell her. Until then, she'll just do her job.

Seth stepped into her room and closed the door for privacy before speaking again.

"I heard about what happened tonight. I'm sorry. There is something we should discuss though, Zarah."

She raised her eyebrows in interest and waited for him to continue. For a few brief loud ticks of her wall clock, she caught his gaze wandering over her body before coming back up to meet her gaze. Luckily she was wearing a full pajama set of flannel pants and a black tank top, rather than something too revealing, or else she would have felt even more uncomfortable the way she was laying on top of her bed with Seth standing nearby.

"With all that is going on now, it might be best if we all just stay in from now on."

"What?" Zarah asked with a frown. "Are you saying no more rounds, no going out of the Compound? Not answering any distress calls?"

Seth nodded, his long, strawberry-blonde hair bouncing slightly with him.

"That's not right!" she nearly shouted, sitting up now. "We have to get out there and help as much as we can. I want humans to understand we're not the enemy."

"And you can't do that if you're killed, either during a raid fight or by a Street Hunter," he tried to reason. His tone was firm and harsh.

She didn't bother arguing further. The tension was building again.

Zarah pointed her finger at the door and hissed.

"Get out of my room now."

Two

After Seth opened the door to walk out, Zarah caught a glimpse of Draven walking by in the hallway. He froze and frowned at her until the door closed, leaving her alone again. She couldn't begin to imagine what he was thinking despite that nothing was going on between her and the Fallen.

The mechanic buzz of the metal shutters closing around the Compound windows sounded off through the building letting her know that sunrise was approaching. Before their move there, they had been in an underground area that didn't require the need for the high-tech shutters to keep the sunlight out, or the dozens of alarms and lock codes to enter and exit. She missed the old building. Times were a bit simpler then.

Zarah wasn't sleeping well. She hadn't in some time, and when she did she kept hoping for another glimpse at her mother. After the incident at the military base when she passed out, she found herself in a dream-state, or perhaps visiting the spirit world, where she had a brief conversation with her. She had yet to tell Thomas about the experience. But Seth knew. Why did she tell him out of all the people around her? She should have told Draven first instead. Keeping it from him too was a decision made from something her mother had told her during their talk.

"Tell Draven to start looking more into his past and family history."

Her mother, Kathleen, had surprised her when saying that but insisted it was important information. She still hadn't hinted to Draven anything about it and decided that she would do all the work herself. Curiosity nagged at her thoughts. Unlike most, he was supposedly not born to a Vampire parent, but had been a full human aged to twenty-two years old before mysteriously waking up late one night as a Vampire and Nathanial at his side to help. Draven always claimed to have hardly any memory of his human life before being turned. Was that really true? Or was he hiding something from everyone? She wanted to learn whatever she could about this questionable past just in case.

    With a huff, she grabbed the book beside her and began trying to concentrate on reading it. She had to get her mind off of things, clear her head, and relax. Most of all, she needed sleep, no matter how bad her body tried to fight against it when hearing the gunshots every so often outside. It took hours before her eyes finally grew heavy and the book landed on her chest.

    Zarah still slept restlessly. Thinking of Draven before falling asleep obviously wasn't good for her. He filled her dreams.

    They were back at the military base after the battle with the Rogues. She was feeding from him and he had a taste that she had never experienced before. She fought the urge from continuing to drink, instead pulling back and looking up into his hypnotizing blue-silver eyes. There was something different about him, not just from the change, but something entirely that she'd never noticed before, and she couldn't place whatever it was that made him stand apart from other

Vampires. Quietly, she lifted her hand and ran her fingers through his thick, shaggy black hair. He smiled down at her, revealing his fangs.

Around them was a silent darkness. A small, radiant white light shined on them like a spotlight. It was not like four months ago when they had been there and bodies lay in heaps of destruction and rubble. Only Draven and her sat there in that moment staring at each other, holding one another, until she broke the silence.

"What is so different?" she whispered. "*You* are different."

He merely shrugged and continued to smile before pulling her closer. Before their lips touched, Seth appeared behind him, standing there in all his Fallen glory beneath another bright glow with his wings spread wide. Zarah turned away from Draven's approaching mouth and stared up at Seth in confusion. He looked back down at her, his gold eyes a storm cloud of emotions and his mouth twisted in sorrow. But Seth couldn't... She reached out to touch his outstretched hand...

Suddenly she dropped from Draven's grasp, hitting hard surface. Draven was gone. Seth was gone.

She awoke on the floor of her small apartment with a groan unwinding the covers from her feet. She wasn't going to even begin trying to make sense of the dream she'd just had.

Climbing back into the bed, she threw a pillow over her until she heard the shutters roll back again as nightfall descended. She still didn't move though. Why bother when Seth probably already told everyone they were all staying in from now on anyway? She just didn't have the energy at the moment to go check to see if it was true. If they were going to go on rounds, someone would come get her. Thirst gnawed at her but she didn't move.

As if reading her mind, someone did barge into her room a few seconds later without bothering to knock. Again. She would have to remember to start locking her door from now on she thought to herself as she frowned, but remained buried beneath her pillows and didn't bother to look up to see who it was. She didn't have to look up to know. His scent was enough.

"Intend on staying in bed all night?"

Zarah heard Draven's tender voice beside the bed. She could picture him smirking down at her as she lay there tangled up in the sheets on her stomach, her hair in disarray, and two pillows haphazardly thrown over her head while her arms dangled at the sides. His usual sweet scent of cherries hit her senses, hinting again at the growing hunger inside her. She slowly rolled over and looked up at him with a tired gaze.

Draven wasn't smirking as she had pictured. His expression was blank, cold. She missed his smile.

"Are we going on rounds?" she asked hoarsely.

He shook his head and then sat down on the bed. He didn't bother for an invitation for that either.

"No. It's been decided that it is probably best for our own safety we should all stay in the confines of the Compound for a while."

"Then why are you even here?" she snapped angrily, yanking her covers from beneath him and laying back down.

"I heard you scream."

Scream? Zarah frowned at her pillow. She didn't remember screaming, but apparently she had when she'd fallen during her dream. Looking over at him again, she no longer saw the coldness, and saw genuine concern as he continued to sit and stare down at her. She swallowed nervously.

"Yeah, I guess I might've. I fell out of bed."
Draven pressed his lips together.
"Zarah, you do know that we are supposed to be a graceful species don't you?"
With that comment, he snickered, and she gasped in mock offense. Using her foot, she playfully shoved him causing another eruption of laughter as he hit the bedpost. She began giggling, too.
As their laughter died down, she continued staring at him. Glad to see that he was smiling, he was as handsome as the day she'd been teamed up with him. Of course, the days that they'd first started working together wasn't on friendly terms in the least bit. They had hated each other at first actually. After

working as partners for some time, they learned there was more to the other than what they thought. During that time, she had also learned he was in a Bonding Pact with her. It had been another one of Nathanial's plans.

A Bonding Pact was a blood-bonding process made between two vampires in which they are bound emotionally and physically. Should she or Draven ever die, the other would feel lost without the other half and eventually starve themselves to end their own life. Most Bonding Pacts were made between lifelong Mates—lovers that knew they wanted to spend their eternity together. Zarah had no choice about the Bonding Pact with Draven.

Shaking her thoughts, she forced a smile back at him.

"Seriously, it was just a bad dream. I'm fine though."

His smile faded and turned back into worry. Suddenly his arm had found its way to resting on the other side of her waist as he leaned over her. Her breath hitched as she tried to ignore the intimate gesture.

"Are you sure? Do you want to talk about the dream?"

"No, it's fine really. You can go. I do need to get up and get dressed so I can grab a drink. Thanks."

She quickly lifted herself from the bed causing him to move back as well. Here was her chance to pull him to her once and for all, and she was pushing him away.

Draven shrugged and stood when she did.

"There's one more thing I wanted to ask you while I was here," he stopped her as she grabbed an armful of clothes from her closet. She turned and looked at him expectantly, waiting for him to continue.

"What's going on between you and Seth?"

Three

"What?" Zarah asked in alarm.

Draven raised his eyebrows, still waiting for an answer.

"Nothing!"
She was beyond yelling at this point. She wanted to clutch him by the shirt collar and punch him in the jaw if it weren't for the fact that it would mess up the face she enjoyed admiring. Instead she clenched her fists at her sides after dropping the clothes into a nearby chair, and glared at him from the doorframe of the closet. There were no jokes in his eyes, and his face had returned to the cold, blank expression as before. He was obviously serious in asking that question.

"Why would you even think that?" she asked, finally calming down enough to speak again.

"I saw you two at the party. And then last night, I saw him coming out of your room. Come on, Zarah.

I'm not stupid. I know that Fallen has it bad for you. Why can't it be possible? Just be honest with me."

She scooped up her clothes again and threw them on the bed before rubbing at her temples due to an oncoming headache. Draven wasn't helping matters either, and his accusations were making her angry.

"Draven, I am being honest. Nothing is going on with Seth. I was simply talking to him at the party. I didn't ask him to kiss me on the cheek, and I've never led him on otherwise. Last night, he came in my room to tell me about how we're all going to be confined to the Compound now and that's it. You're taking things out of proportion."

"Alright," he said softly.

His tone didn't change things though. Zarah was mad. She looked up at him and hissed, baring her fangs.

"Even so, if there *was* something going on, it wouldn't be your business. Would it? It's not like we're a couple either."

A low growl erupted from him and he headed for the door.

"You're absolutely right."

When the door slammed, she let out a frustrated scream and threw her book at it. Yelping, she picked it up and stroked the cover apologetically. It was a copy of William Shakespeare's *A Midsummer Night's Dream*—one of her favorites.

"I'm sorry. I shouldn't abuse such good literature, even if I am angry," she said out loud before laying it gently down on a nearby table.

All the while she got dressed, she couldn't help but think how close he had been to her on the bed. The first time in months, he had smiled, joked, and leaned over her. What does she do? Push him back away. Maybe it wasn't him after all being the distant one pulling back, stopping. Maybe it was her.

No. He'd had his chances plenty of times to move anything forward if he'd wanted. She'd given him opportunities. After the party even, she tried approaching him alone in his room only for him to shun her.

"Hey."

She walked in, closing the door behind her, and sat on his bed. He was standing at his window looking out over the city.

As she kicked off her shoes, she let out a short laugh and started playing around with a remote.

"Come on, Draven. You can't stare out the window all night. Let's watch a movie or something. We have all these neat gadgets now." The sound blared to life over the speakers and she began to flip through a screen to choose a movie.

"No."

His abrupt, harsh tone hit her, and caused her to stop. She turned back to face him and found him looking at her. His gaze was dark, unhappy. Her smile faded as she slowly sat up from her position.

"What?" she asked in confusion.

"I don't want to. I think it's best you just go. You should have a room next door ready for you."

With narrowed eyes and an angry huff, she threw the remote at him—which, of course, he'd caught effortlessly—and gathered her shoes before stomping out of his room. She also may have let a few curses fly at him along the way.

Later, thinking he had simply been in a bad mood over the fight or the party, or just something recent, she had tried again two weeks later only to get a similar result. It had become apparent that he just didn't want to be around her. Perhaps he didn't want her at all, and she quit trying. She distanced her emotions and only began working with him when necessary from that point. So maybe he had distanced himself from her after all, but she had done the same, too.

So, why couldn't she forget him? His laugh echoed in her mind and his smile played on repeat in her dreams. Whenever she smelled cherries, she thought of him. When a cheesy horror movie came on, he was on her mind. She knew those were his favorites, and on some nights when she felt particularly down, she'd put one on just for the sake of a laugh or smile—even though he didn't watch them with her anymore.

Tying her boot laces, a tear escaped and slid down her cheek. Snorting in disbelief at her weakness, she quickly wiped it away when a knock came at her door.

"Yeah?" After her voice stuttered, she took a moment to cough and clear her throat.

"Hey, Sunshine."

Zarah looked up to see Seth standing above her and nearly gaped. He was shirtless, wearing only baggy jeans, and smiling down at her. She quickly clamped her mouth shut and frowned. Could it be true what Draven had said earlier? Did Seth like her? If it was, she really didn't know what to think of that yet.

"You look like hell, you know that?" He joked when she didn't say anything.

"Oh, that's what every woman wants to hear. Be still my barely-beating heart." She responded sarcastically, standing. Beside him, she didn't quite reach his shoulders. He let out a loud laugh and something strangely fluttered inside her. He had a nice, energetic laugh, and it made her want to smile.

Studying him carefully, she noted the glittering gold in his eyes that twinkled when he was happy. They changed constantly with his emotions. She slowly found herself wondering what else he was like, the things he was interested in, and what made him *Seth*. Only on friendly terms, of course.

"So…what is it?" she finally asked after an awkward silence. Her voice came out raspy and she had to clear her throat with a cough.

As if suddenly remembering his reason for coming into her room, he snapped his fingers and nodded.
"Oh right. The guys want to work on some training tonight. I was sent in here to tell you that they'll be in the gym whenever you're ready."
She nodded while crossing the room to her vanity to start brushing through her hair. The tangles in her long mess were making things difficult and every few seconds she winced.
"I'll be there as soon as I'm done getting a drink, thanks."

Seth continued to stand behind her at a comfortable distance. He looked to be considering something else to say. She stopped brushing and raised her eyebrows in silent question, waiting for him to continue.

"Have any more dreams lately?"

His question made Zarah tense. Glancing at him through the mirror's reflection, she remembered last night's dream where he had made his appearance behind Draven. She remembered the wings…and the hurt expression on his face as he stared down at the two of them holding each other. But something odd happened there, she felt compelled to let go of Draven and try to reach out for Seth. That was when she fell. The dream had felt so real.

Slowly, she shook her head. "No," she lied and returned to brushing out her hair.

When it was tame, she set the brush down and began to head for the door, hoping he would follow. Instead he grabbed her arm and pulled her back.

"Please don't lie to me, Zarah. I can see it in your face. If you don't want to talk about it, that's fine.

But don't lie." His eyes were soft, sincere and pleading as they scanned her face. He held onto her arm lightly.

She pulled away.

"Alright. Fine. I don't want to talk about it. It was just a dream, okay? Nothing to worry about. If I have more Mom moments though, I'll let you know."

He nodded. "I'll accept that then."

"Speaking of Mom moments…I should really tell Thomas soon. See you later, Seth," she added before she continued out of the room and toward the kitchen, as he followed out and headed to the gym in the opposite direction.

Four

Despite the constantly-growing war, the Compound still had a good stock of bagged and bottled blood for the Guardians. Zarah knew it wouldn't last forever though. It was going to be problem when they ran out and would have to hunt for the first time in decades. Under normal circumstances, they ran scams of blood donor drives to get human blood without the need of actually hunting. Things weren't normal anymore. They could no longer do that without suspicion. Even humans who really did try to run a blood drive were taken in by the Hunters for questioning now.

Zarah grabbed a bottle from the refrigerator and started drinking. Taking in long gulps, she hadn't realized how thirsty she had been until she had it. When was the last time she'd fed? A couple of days ago at least. Everyone was trying to ration themselves to make the stock last as long as possible. Some of the Guardians were only taking drinks a couple days a week. It was definitely going to be a growing problem.

They would get weak. She knew they should all be at their full strength, always prepared for anything.

Without any guilt, she drank down a second bottle before discarding both, and headed toward the gym to meet up with the others. On the short walk through the hallway, she silently hoped that Draven wouldn't be present at training.

"It took you long enough."

Unfortunately she didn't always get what she wanted. He was standing by the door when she stepped inside. Taking a moment to glare at him before turning back to stare around the gym, she found that everyone had gathered and she really was the last to arrive. Even the Fallen were there, casually standing against the far wall and visiting amongst each other. Seth looked up as if he had sensed her presence and waved enthusiastically. If she had one way to describe it, it looked kind of ridiculous. Like an overgrown child. His large hand flapped side-to-side wildly in the air and he had a huge grin pasted on his face. She suppressed a laugh. What kind of human movies had he been watching to learn from? She returned the wave with hesitation and forced a soft smile. Draven let out a snort of disgust beside her.

"See, I told you. Exiled Boy has it bad for you."

Zarah spun and stared at him incredulously. "I have no idea what you're talking about, but you need to just drop it already."

She spoke low and through clenched teeth with a hard, threatening edge to her voice. She didn't want to stand there and argue with him in front of everyone so she stood close, pretending to have a private, soft conversation instead. He stood with his arms crossed at his chest, peering down at her in mock amusement, and shrugged. She wanted to reach up and slap the look off his face as her anger rolled into waves again.

With a frustrated growl, she turned away in time to see Thomas approaching with his mate, Alyssa, and managed to fake a grin.

"Hey sis, what took you so long?"

"Oh, a little slow moving tonight I guess. I had to stop by the kitchen, too. Are we ready?"

Thomas nodded and reached for Alyssa's hand as they made their way toward the center of the gym. Draven walked beside her in silence. Oftentimes, no matter how many others she was surrounded by in the Compound, Zarah felt lonely. Her brother had his mate, who was the only other female in the building at the current time but not particularly sociable, the Fallen had each other, and the Guardians were all good friends. Even with the changes, she still felt like the same outcast she had always been.

Two of the original Fallen had left shortly after their arrival to the new Compound, wanting to go back to their own mates wherever that had been. So now they were down to six Fallen and seven Guardians living in the Compound, each one having their own separate apartment. The building was several stories. The rooms along with a lounge that had a game room and attached kitchen were on the top floor. The gym occupied much of the floor below. On the first two stories were a hidden garage and weapons storage, and extra rooms for future additions if needed. While it wasn't as private as the old underground Compound had been, it was still comfortable living for the large group.

Through the last four months, Zarah had managed to learn more about the Fallen, including their names. There was Seth, of course, who seemed to be a bit like their leader. Or it appeared that way since he made most of their decisions and they followed in everything he said. Then there was Aiden, Landon, Cam, Daniel, and Heath. Albeit all sharing the same trait of bright gold eyes and massive black wings, they were each unique in their own way still. They also never shared full names. Something about it being sacred to them. She didn't fully understand that part yet.

    One was loud, always prepared for a fight and had a bit of a temper—that was Cam. His wild, shaggy blue hair matched his personality. He was fun to be around though and always knew when someone needed to be cheered up. Landon and Daniel were mostly quiet and reserved. They were twin brothers, both with short cropped black hair but with notable differences. Landon had neon green highlights in his hair, and Daniel had bright red highlights and facial hair subtly growing along his chin. Despite their loud appearances, they kept mostly to the sidelines, only speaking when necessary or spoken to, and watched a lot of television. She only assumed they might be good listeners if needed, but never really talked much with the twins. Heath was emotionless. Rarely smiling, cold and distant. He was shorter than the others but more toned. His white-blonde hair fell straight, thin and long just past his shoulders. Seth had told Zarah once that Heath's closed behavior was due to an event in his past. He'd lost his mate several years ago due to Rogues and didn't carry a particular fondness to Vampires in general. Still, he hung around at Seth's request and he was an amazing fighter. Zarah intended on getting to know him better with time.

  They could easily pass for humans in their early twenties when their wings were magically hidden away. Except for Aiden. He was the oldest, and the oldest looking, with a more mature-defined face that would have led someone to think he was more along in his early thirties. Aiden had quickly become an acquaintance of sorts when they'd found they shared a love of old literature and began swapping books over the last few weeks to pass the hours between rounds. He was Seth's cousin, too, sharing a similar strawberry-blonde hair color but trimmed in a more old-fashioned, short style and constantly kept neat.

  The Guardians she knew well from her time in and out as a fighter. After the Compound was raided and destroyed by Rogues, not many survived. Markus, Jerry, James, Nicolas and Brayden remained with them. She thought of them as brothers now after growing closer to them through the days. Funny enough, they used to fear her, hate her. But things had changed. Namely the world and all of them along with it. They were certainly excited to have Thomas back, too.

As they gathered in a large circle at the center of the gym, she glanced around the room at everyone.

"I think we should address an issue first before we get started."

Their attention held onto her and she cleared her throat nervously. Making sure to put things as delicately as possible, she tried the best approach to the subject by being blunt and to the point.

"Quit rationing your drinks. If we run out of our stock, we'll just have to risk it and start hunting again like the Vampires we are."

The Guardians gasped and the Fallen frowned in disapproval. Sure they would, those boys didn't need blood to survive. That was another thing to the list about them she hadn't figured out also. How did they get sustenance? She didn't even see them eat food, and only have the occasional drink—alcoholic type drinks.

"You can't be serious," Draven whispered harshly beside her, getting her attention again. She suddenly realized that every pair of eyes in the room were on her, unblinking.

"I'm very serious. We have to be at our full capabilities, not weak and hungry. Also, how do we know how far we can push our power if we're constantly starved?" she argued.

"She's right. We can't do anything if we're weak."

Zarah looked over at her brother and smiled in relief at his support. Within minutes of him stepping forward in agreement, the others began nodding along as well. Although the Fallen didn't seem thrilled with the discussion, it wasn't theirs to discuss.

"Alright, let's get to work," she said as they began pairing up, getting into teams, or going off on their own for their work-outs. Some of the Fallen took a couple of the Guardians to work with their new elemental power since their recent changes.

Zarah set off alone again. She crossed the gym and sat down to begin stretching. A few minutes later, Guardians across the gym started playing around with their elemental powers, and it became loud with the buzz of laughter and shouts of surprise. She didn't move. It had been Jerry's idea after the battle at the military base for them all to be Changed after learning about the power she possessed. At that point, she had already changed Draven when saving his life from another attack. Her blood was special. Any who drank from her would change and gain an Elemental power. The cycle continued from there—if one drank from a Changed One, they would change as well. Slowly, they were becoming a new race.

Watching them in the gym as they were still trying to learn their power by building it up at will and throw it out where needed held her attention for a while. Zarah wasn't up to practicing that night though. Instead she kept to basic physical training and continued stretching her tired muscles.

Someone turned on a stereo and started blasting heavy metal. Probably Cam. Not that Zarah minded the music at all, some of her favorite tunes echoed out through the loud speakers. It was just disheartening when you could still hear the gunshots and military vehicles rumbling by outside even over the music.

"Are you not practicing tonight?"

Thomas had approached quietly and interrupted her thoughts. She looked up at him and grimaced, shaking her head.

"No, I'm not really in the mood. I think I'll just go in the other room and pound on the bags for a while." She started to stand and head to the adjacent room where they kept some more equipment, such as punching bags, extra weights, and boards for knife throwing.

"Are you alright?"

She sighed in frustration as she put on her padded, fingerless gloves for her work-out and slipped out of her boots. She hadn't dressed for boxing but didn't care.

"I'm fine," she mumbled and started to walk away. Thomas pulled her back, protesting.

"You know, it's kind of a given that as my sister, I automatically know when you're lying. Come on, now. Be honest."

Zarah turned back to him with a frown.
"You know I'm getting really sick of being asked if I'm alright. No, things aren't okay, but I'll be fine. So, let's drop it."
She glanced around the room, noting that Draven stood close by and probably could hear part of their conversation if he tried. Annoyed, she gave her attention back to Thomas. He must have noticed her brief gaze because he was looking in the same direction she had been before meeting her eyes again.

"Is this about you and him? I thought you two were—" he started in confusion.
"No. We're not and it's not," she quickly cut him off. The pain in her chest though reminded her that part of her problem was Draven, but she wasn't about to confess that to her brother. He'd just implied

that he thought they were a couple, which shocked her momentarily. She wondered how many others thought the same thing.

Thomas suddenly nodded as if an idea occurred to him. "It's about last night then, isn't it? That raid on the Hiders?"

She narrowed her eyes.
"You weren't in that house, Thomas. You didn't see that awful scene. It's not just about last night, but everything that's been going on. We're at war now. I've had a lot on my mind lately."
Her brother slowly nodded in agreement. She faced the wall, pretending to be stretching her legs again so she wouldn't have to look at him directly, trying to speak as softly as she could in hopes that others wouldn't overhear their discussion.
"All of my life, I've always been taught to protect humans. Now, in order to survive, it looks like I'm going to have to fight them. Tell me something, do you believe what they say on television is true? That if Vampires win, we'll rule over them and treat them like slaves?"

"I'm not sure," he stuttered in a shocked whisper.

"Well, I think you are. We all know it will happen. Why? Because thousands of our kind out there are supporters and always have been. They've been waiting for this kind of opportunity," she said matter-of-factly, straightening up. "Either way, bro, this world is in for some serious dark times ahead. Whether we win or lose."

With that, she strolled away and into the adjacent workroom, leaving her brother in a stunned silence.

Five

Hitting the punching bag always relieved stress for Zarah. That night was no exception. As her fists exploded into the soft foam hanging down in front of her, she reveled in each strike. She was so lost in her thoughts she hadn't heard the door open and someone enter the room behind her.

"Everyone is leaving the gym now."
Jumping at the sound of Draven's voice, she spun and faced him before regaining her composure.
"So?"
She went back to the punching bag, trying to ignore his presence as he stepped further into the room and approached.
"So…take a break. No sense in wasting what energy you do have."

"I'm fine," she repeated what seemed to be becoming a track that sounded like it was skipping.

He shrugged, rolling his eyes, and began to walk away. She thought he was done and leaving, until he suddenly grabbed her, causing a shriek to escape. With a single yank and toss, he flipped her easily over his head and onto her back as she landed roughly on the blue mat on the floor.

 Zarah groaned, rubbing her back momentarily, before staring up in angered shock as he stood above her impatiently. He crossed his arms over his chest and raised his eyebrows.

 "Any other time, I wouldn't have been able to do that, and you know it."

 "That's not fair! I thought you were leaving so I wasn't even paying attention!" she yelled, starting to stand. Her cheeks burned, flushing pink with fury. He stood in front of her in silence.

 She threw her hand back and prepared to slap him but he caught it quickly. Raging further, she tried to reach with the other, only for him to grab that one as well. Beyond irritation, she was simply blinded by only wanting to get at least one hit in and tried to kick.

He threw out his leg and tripped her, causing her to flip back on the mat again with a loud growl.

"Like I said, take a break."

He left, stepping over her as she continued to lie in the floor, smirking on his way out.

"Punk," she mumbled when she slowly rose to her feet, noting that her muscles were sore. He laughed, hearing her remark, before the door closed to leave her alone again.

Unfortunately, he was right. She needed a break and rest. Yanking her gloves off, she threw them across the room in a fit and stormed out of the room. She shook her head in disbelief at the tears stinging her eyes. God, she was acting so human it was disgusting. Driven by her emotions. What was wrong with her? Was she developing some sort of late teenage hormone thing, despite the fact that she wasn't technically a human teenager anymore? She was stuck at the age of nineteen forever, and had been a Vampire for almost forty years now. So, what was the deal?

"You look deep in thought, Sunshine."

Zarah had been deep in thought as always. She hadn't heard Seth come walking up beside her until he spoke, using the nickname for her that he had seemed to pick up over the last couple of weeks. Where he got it from, she had no idea. Of course, Vampires couldn't go out in the daylight. The Fallen could during certain times, mostly if the sun wasn't at its highest point, like at dawn or dusk, and in a way she was jealous of that. She remembered trying to see the sun briefly a while ago at sunrise when her and Draven were trying to make it back to the old Compound in time. The light had practically chased them along the way but she still turned back for a curious glance. Even through the window and shade, just staring at the light had mildly burned her eyes.

She continued walking but laughed softly. "Yeah, you know me. Deep philosophical thoughts as always."

He grinned, looking a little goofy, and walked with her. "I always figured you silently pondered things like that. The whole universe thing, I mean, we are just a speck in the vast system, right?"

That time Zarah let out a loud giggle and playfully shoved his shoulder. She didn't know what it was, but Seth always seemed to know how to bring her back up from a down mood even if it was just temporary.

"I have no idea what you're talking about," she joked, still smiling. They walked into the Lounge together and she instinctively looked around for Draven, relieved to find he wasn't there. Annoyingly though, Seth continued to follow her around trying to talk. She ignored him half the time, not hearing most of the things he was saying.

When she sat down on a couch by one of the large bay windows, he was still talking. She started to lean her head back and close her eyes.

"...Masters are getting curious, and their curiosity is dangerous."

Snapping her eyes open again, she looked at him in confusion. He was seated across from her in a plush chair, drinking a glass of wine, and had lost his joking manner.

"What did you just say?" she asked harshly.

He frowned his disapproval, realizing that she obviously hadn't been listening.

"I said, the word is getting around. Fallen Masters are getting curious about you and trust me, their curiosity is dangerous. Not to be taken lightly. If you think this situation with the humans is bad, you haven't seen much yet."

"You know what I'm curious about, Seth?" Her eyebrows were raised, not seemingly the slightest bit worried about his warning. He glanced at her with a scowl.

"Your species. Here I thought Vampires were a mysterious bunch, but boy was I wrong when I met you guys. I know absolutely nothing about the Fallen other than the power you possess."

"Are you trying to imply something?"

"*No*," she emphasized sarcastically. "I'm simply saying that maybe it's time you and your group open up a bit. Tell us more about your kind. I'd particularly like to know more about my mother at least."

He sighed and leaned back in his seat.

"Were you taught nothing in your training, Sunshine? We learned everything about Vampires during ours."

"Like what?"

"The three branches—Guardians, Hiders, and Rogues. How the war began between our species over three centuries ago, the turning processes, skills you possessed, and your weaknesses." He listed nonchalantly, beginning to look bored. She frowned and stood.

"Obviously we are on different paths. So you owe us the favor of giving the information we should have about you. I can't fight these so-called Masters and their Warriors you speak of blindly."

Seth jumped to his feet and grabbed her hand, startling her beyond more words. His eyes were bright and fierce, but full of a tenderness she had yet seen from him until that moment.

"You will never fight them, Zarah, because you would lose. No matter how much I prepared you."

Six

Zarah walked toward her small apartment in a slight daze. After the meeting with Seth, things became awkward. She had departed from the Lounge in a rush after his statement without saying anything else. He'd tried to call out to her but she just waved him off and continued on her way. She hadn't wanted to hear anything else from him.

The night in the Compound was growing quiet as the hours grew later and others started to prepare for bed. Hallways were empty. She welcomed the silence during her walk around the building, the only sound being her boots echoing off the tiles. The vision of her mother kept nagging at her—it had been months since she dreamed of her—and as she turned down the hall that led to her brother's living area, she knew what she had to do.

It may take her awhile to get many answers from Seth about their race and more information about her mother's life and death, but the least she could do is tell Thomas about the dream at last. Maybe he could even help if he knew anything also.

After softly knocking on the door, it swung open and she was met with her brother's smiling face. A television was on somewhere in the room, sounding like it was tuned to some high-action movie with a lot of gun shots and police sirens in the background.

"Hey, Sis. Come on in and watch the movie with me. I feel like since we've been back, we hardly speak."

Thomas reached out and tugged her into the room as she forced a smile. It was true; they hardly spent much time together outside of work or practice in the gym. In truth, she was still trying build her relationship back with him, but first felt that she needed closure on her own volatile emotions that she harbored for so long after he had turned her Rogue two years prior. Growing up with him had been different. They were always close, more like best friends rather than siblings. Like most children born to a vampire parent, they'd had extreme sensitivity to sunlight and had to be privately tutored rather than attend school. Most people would have assumed this would cause a lot of trouble between the siblings, but that situation only made them closer.

"What movie?"

"I don't even know to be honest, but it's entertaining," he replied with a laugh as they stepped into the apartment, Zarah shutting the door behind her.

She slipped her boots off and left them in the narrow hall that led from the door and opened up into the living room before following him. Before taking a seat, she looked around to see that like always, everything was neat and organized. Thomas was constantly about being tidy and she picked on him often about the obsession.

The bedroom, across from them, was left open showing a large spacious area with a king-size bed—again neatly made—with luxurious burgundy blankets and thick white carpet. In the living area, the same plush carpet was soft beneath her feet as she sat on a brown leather wrap-around couch. A beautiful amber-colored Tiffany lamp sat on a nearby table, dimly lighting the room. Her brother fell in beside her and they stared silently at the television across from them for several long, awkward silent minutes.

Everyone in the Compound had an apartment in this layout—a living room with one bedroom and a full bathroom. Except they could style it to their liking. Unlike at the old one, they no longer had their own kitchen area, allowing for more space, and had to go to The Lounge where the public kitchen area was located at for any needs. Thomas and Alyssa loved clean, organized, and sophisticated looks. She found the style of their apartment fitting for them.

"Where is Alyssa?" she finally asked, turning to him.

"She's at the gym again. She wanted some time in there alone because she feels so rusty in all of her skills."

Zarah nodded her understanding, and began nervously shaking her leg.

"Look Thomas, about earlier... I'm—" she started, only for him to pat her shoulder while shaking his head and interrupting.

"There is no need for you to apologize."

"Yes, there is. I need to tell you something and it's really hard for me to say it so just shut up for a few minutes please." Zarah snapped at him then leaned forward and started rubbing her temples with a sigh. Her brother sat forward, confused, and turned the television off.

"What is it?" he asked, ignoring her request to be quiet. She let it slide and continued on in silence for another moment.

"I saw Mom."

She blurted it so fast while her head was buried in her hands that it came out muffled. When Thomas said nothing, she looked up to see his expression a mixture of shock and puzzlement. Unsure he'd heard the first time, she repeated herself again.

"You saw Mom? What do you mean, Zarah?" he asked. "How long ago?"

His voice was rising and she could sense the anger coming in now.

"It was a dream I had the night we came here after the warehouse fight. She came to me in this stunning vision, telling me how there were going to be changes in the world, changes with me and to take care of you. She said she wasn't destroyed by Rogues, but by the Fallen Masters and their Warriors, and that I would learn more in due time. I was left with a lot of questions, Thomas." Zarah explained quickly, deciding at last minute to leave out the information about their mother's inclination to look into Draven's past.

He breathed slowly and she could tell he was trying to calm himself.

"Why didn't you tell me before?"

"I'm not sure, to be honest. I didn't know how to tell you."

"Are you sure it wasn't just a dream—that it was real?"

Slowly, she nodded.

"When I told Seth, he said it was very possible for her to come to me in that vision due to our link and her still being a part of the spirit realm—" she began, but Thomas shot up from the couch and glared at her in a rage.

"You told the Fallen, but you couldn't tell me?"

"Come on, don't get mad. I didn't know who else to talk to about it at the time and he knew her! I thought maybe he could help me understand, and it's possible he still can. I didn't tell him about the vision—only that I saw her and asked if it could be real. I wanted to make sure I wasn't going crazy from all these weird changes going on!"

She was standing then, shouting back at him as tears stung her eyes. She hated that the waterworks had hit again but having her brother mad at her when she was only trying to tell him the truth upset her. She guessed that was a sign that she was trying after all to mend things with him and his feelings toward her were important.

Thomas must have seen the tears or felt the sincerity, she didn't know, because suddenly without any warning he grabbed her and pulled her into a fierce, tight hug. It knocked the wind out of her.

"It's fine. We'll forget it. You've told me now and that's what matters," he whispered. Slowly she brought her arms around his back and hugged him in return.

"Thomas, why am I such a freak?"

She was still wrapped tightly in his embrace, her words tumbling out in barely a whisper against his cheek as her lips trembled. It was one of the rare occurrences she let her walls down, showing how vulnerable she could be.

Her brother pulled away from her and shook his head.

"You are not a freak. Never."

She forced a smile and tried to protest.

"Of course you can say that. You're my brother. Why couldn't I have taken more after Dad like you obviously did?"

"I would say it even if I weren't your brother, Zarah. You're special, and you will be something great to this world. I'm sure of it."

She looked into his eyes and saw only a stern expression. He wasn't joking, he wasn't saying any of it just to try and make her feel better, he was telling her what he believed to be the truth. Remaining silent, she nodded in understanding before turning away and bending down to grab her boots from the hallway.

"We'll see about that," she replied with a soft laugh.

Alyssa strolled in as Zarah prepared to leave. Her brother's Mate was often soft-spoken and not very sociable, but she was an excellent fighter when needed. She greeted her with a nod while walking past, giving Thomas a fast kiss on the cheek, then going into the bedroom and shutting the door. Zarah made a mental note to spend some time with Alyssa one day personally. After all, she was the only other female in the Compound, and being her brother's Mate, she would like to get to know her better. Thomas had chosen Alyssa shortly before going Rogue. Alyssa disappeared not long afterward. It was proven the night that her brother returned to warn her about the Rogues when Zarah first paired up with Draven a few months ago that she had gone Rogue with him back then so that they could stay together.

"I thought you were going to stay and watch the movie?"

She smiled.

"Sorry, I have some things I want to do before I go to bed. I promise we'll get in some sibling time soon, though."

He returned her smile and nodded in understanding.

"Alright. I'll meet you at the gym later. And if you have any more dreams, don't hesitate next time to come to me."

Seven

The hallways were deserted by the time Zarah had left Thomas' apartment. Sunrise was already on its way again and she could hear the automatic steel shutters closing around the building. Outside, the world was starting its day. Humans were braving the early light of dawn, thankful for the new day she was sure. She cursed the sun, wishing she could go out during the hours when it was almost peaceful, when she hardly heard any of the military trucks rumbling by or the guns going off.

Stupid human literature had been right about one thing at least—they couldn't be out during daylight, and they rejoiced in that, using that time to get their work done or make new plans. Her team stayed in The Compound and continued watching the news regularly for updates. There was nothing new really. The world was in a mass panic. In the short time since the warehouse and Nathanial's death, countries had banded together or shut down completely, and Vampires became the hunted.

They never even had the chance to tell them they once protected them. And now, there would be no way to even get them to listen.

The U.S. was the worst. The President had sent orders around to all military personnel to kill once confirmed by any means they wanted. Some of those officers liked to play cruel games. She had never thought humans to be such a harsh race until now. But Zarah's sympathy still showed for others. The country was in turmoil, slowly rotting away into a power-hungry nation where everyone became afraid for their lives, not just from the Vampires, but from poverty. Businesses were forced to close. People were forced from their homes. The military and government were beginning to control everything.

The world was falling to pieces around them all.

Seeing all of the growing destruction and devastation, thoughts rolled around her constantly. One occurred to her most prominently that she had discussed with Thomas earlier. Would it be so much worse if Vampires jumped into war and ruled the humans after all? Depending on who the ruler over all was that is...

The raid from a couple nights ago still raged through her. Things were already growing worse. Something needed to be done, and she was stuck.

She paused in front of Draven's door. It was closed, but she could hear his stereo blasting through the walls. After starting to raise her hand to knock, she changed her mind and turned away instead.

When she went into the main office of the new Compound, exhaustion was taking a toll, but she wanted to look through the files while she still had an idea at the forefront of her mind. The office was small, near the lobby and was never occupied by anyone in particular. The door stayed open but important documents were locked away in steel cabinets behind the big oak desk. Only she and Draven had access to the key that works the cabinets and locked desk drawers. As she stepped up to a wall panel that appeared to be wood, she slid back a small square to reveal a hidden space. Behind it was a safe. She rolled through the combination with ease.

After opening, she peered in, staring at a few stacks of money, some jewels they had picked up at various homes after humans had raided and killed the others, a gun she had placed there for safe keeping, and the set of keys.

Zarah kept the keys after opening the file cabinets, stashing them away into her pocket instead of returning them to safe. She didn't know why, but it just felt better holding on to them.

There weren't many files left. Most of them had been destroyed during the fire a few months ago at the previous building. Nathanial hadn't kept them in a safe box, and instead they had been in his office in a wooden chest. When they first arrived at their new location, a few of the other Guardians had gone back one evening to shift through the rubble and debris for anything they could use. They brought back the surviving files, guns and ammunition, and some of their personal belongings from the apartments there.

Zarah had lost all of her clothing with the exception of what she'd been wearing that night. At least she still had her favorite pair of boots.

Going through the few files, she hoped that Draven's had survived at least. Maybe Nathanial had known something about him that they didn't and put it there. Maybe that's why he ordered the Bonding Pact last year when she was curing as a Rogue—some kind of connection already? Her mother was adamant about her finding information about him. Manila folders slid through her hands—some wrinkled and bent with papers sticking out messily. Some with burnt corners—as she scanned the tabs at the names. Hers and Thomas' file was there, both half charred with yellow-stained and burned papers, but she didn't have time to stop and go through those folders. She might come back to them a different time. There was only a small stack so it was quick, and she let out a breath of relief when she finally saw Draven's name on one of them, pulling it to the top of the pile.

Her rush of relief quickly turned to disappointment and frustration when she opened the file and found only two papers inside. Nothing more than that. There wasn't a certificate of birth or documentation on his parents or even place of residence before he came to be a Guardian. Zarah frowned. She pulled up the first paper for inspection, only to find that it was his contract with Nathanial about the Bonding Pact. His signature at the bottom was beautiful with wide, elegant loops, and she caught herself staring at the writing for several long seconds before setting it aside.

The second paper was something else, and a bit more suspicious. It was a record of when Draven arrived to the Compound, and a picture that had been scanned and printed beneath the brief information. He was lying in a hospital bed with tubes running into his arms, pumping blood into his body. Zarah could see the picture was of him during his change, between the stages of human and vampire. Yet she didn't understand why Nathanial had even recorded that in the first place. It confused her. As she started to pick up the paper for closer inspection, she noticed it felt heavy, weighted down in the back and turned it over. Taped in the middle was a small memory stick for a USB. She pulled it off and pocketed it, curious at its contents. There wasn't time to connect it to the computer in the office. Someone was coming.

In a rush, she shoved the files back in place and locked everything away again. After the last drawer closed and she began to head toward the door, Draven passed. He stopped when he saw her and frowned.

"What were you doing in there?" His tone was suspicious. She shrugged, her face neutral and calm.

"I was counting our funds," she lied. He narrowed his eyes and regarded her for several silent seconds before it seemed he accepted her response.

"Whatever. It doesn't matter anyway. You can't go out right now, and that means for anything."

"I know that," she snapped and began to push past him. "But eventually we'll have no choice, and we'll need to be prepared. We can't be held up here for eternity."

Zarah kept her head down, hiding her face through her long mess of auburn hair, while she continued down the hallway and into her room. She didn't want to be in his presence right then. The USB drive pushed against her hip in the depth of her pocket with each step. He didn't seem to care about her hurrying off anyway as he moved on toward the kitchen.

Once inside her room, she bolted the locks and looked around. There was clutter everywhere. Thomas would call it a "pig-sty", but she called it lived-in. It wasn't like there was dust all over the place or dirty laundry hanging over her chairs. She just didn't exactly organize the way he did. She liked to pile her craft supplies around in various spots of the room, or books lay strewn about, but she knew where everything was by the end of the night.

The new Compound building had larger rooms for the residents. She had an attached balcony, but in recent days it stayed locked and closed off due to the building war. Since there was an open kitchen in the Lounge, the room didn't have one like her old one did. Instead, she now had a small office space with a desk and laptop, and a larger living room area with a plush beige sofa and wall-mounted flat screen television. Her bed was separated by a partial wall near the couch, and sat close to the balcony windows. It was a beautiful four-post king size with sheer, purple drapery. She rarely made her bed too. Her brother always sneered at her when he came into her room and saw that.

After changing into comfortable clothes, she walked over to her desk with the new-found memory stick. Her computer hummed to life when she sat down and pushed the power button. Staring at the small piece of plastic warily, she plugged it into the port and watched her screen, waiting for whatever it was to come up.

"Is this thing on?" A video flashed on her screen and a familiar voice came through her speaker. Zarah froze, frightened, watching the images come slowly into focus.

"Yes, sir," another distant voice to an unseen face answered.

"Okay, good. Now get out."

She watched, leaning forward, while the video shook and forms began to take shape. A body began to come into view. She could now see a hospital room in the background, and a bed with a pale hand hanging from the side. The camera was obviously being set onto a stand so that it could take its video hands-free. She saw the operator and swallowed back a surprised scream.

The video had been filmed by Nathanial. And when he panned the screen to the hospital bed behind him, she saw who was laying there. Draven.

It was similar to the same scene she'd seen in the picture in his file. He lay unconscious on a table as Nathanial walked around the room readying some equipment—pulling out bags of blood and needles.

The wings were the most shocking surprise though. She hadn't expected *that*.

Her hand came to her mouth in shocked horror, trembling, when she saw the magnificent, black feathers splayed out behind his back. Nathanial stood beside the bed and was staring at the camera with a silent, malicious smile as if he knew she'd be watching this someday.

Eight

Draven had been Fallen once. Zarah stared at her screen in shock and continued to force herself to watch the video. Nathanial wasn't talking, but she learned enough.

The Vampire she knew today hadn't been human before his turning. Not only that, he'd been tortured. He'd been an experiment.

She watched on helplessly as the video continued. Nathanial reached for a dagger. In a silver flash, the wings were shredded from Draven's back, and she gasped out loud. Her stomach churned when they fell to the floor in a bloody heap. She was silently thankful that he had been unconscious during that awful procedure.

"The subject's name is Draven Kinsley. He is approximately twenty-two years old and Unclaimed."

Zarah frowned in confusion. She didn't know what the term "Unclaimed" meant. Did it mean that he didn't have a mate? Or that he was an Exiled One like Seth and the others? She'd have to find a way to ask about this.

Nathanial continued working on Draven's unconscious form in the video. Needles that pumped blood into his system were taped at the crook of his elbow. Tubes connected to IV bags. Her old boss moved away from him and picked up the discarded, bloody wings now on the floor. Blood streaked across the white tiles from the black feathers where they dragged behind him as he made his way to the trash chute at the other end of the hospital room, but he ignored the mess. When he was finished shoving them down the metal bin, he turned back to the camera and folded his hands in front of him. She knew the video had been made many years before; it had very poor color and quality. He must've later used his computer program to get it onto the memory stick. She didn't understand a lot of the newer technology.

"This Fallen was found in the yard of the Duncan's after Kathleen's death. He was badly injured after a fight that I believe was meant to try and save

Zarah's mother. By morning he will be changed into a Vampire, the scars from his removed wings will be gone, and he will not remember anything. This should be interesting."

She threw her chair back as if she'd been struck herself and jumped away. Of course she'd known that he'd been turned before she joined the Guardians with Thomas, but this was beyond shocking. The information presented told her that the events led on a domino train through time. Her mother's death led to Draven's change, led to Zarah and Thomas joining the team, led to their ambush and Thomas being turned Rogue, and so on. Her mouth went dry and hands began to tremble. She took slow steps back to the computer, staring at it like a piece of foreign equipment, with Nathanial's sick smile staring back at her from the screen. How had Nathanial found Draven at her house to begin with anyway?

As if answering her question, the door behind him opened and her eyes bulged. She hadn't seen the man since he went rabid on his thirst for vengeance, though there he was obviously still clinging to his sanity.

It was her father.

"Did you finish your son's turning?" Nathanial asked him, distracted by the entrance. He forgot the camera.

Her father, William, nodded, and turned his attention toward Draven. He frowned.

"What's this? I thought you said you were going to take care of him? This looks awful," William started in frantic worry, making long strides toward the bed. She swallowed back forming tears. Her father's tall, muscular form towered above Nathanial's slender frame, but he was too lost in thought and didn't see what was going on behind him.

Nathanial had a small needle in his hand with a red-hued liquid. He was approaching slowly from behind.

"I think we could use a new Guardian, William. Don't you agree? Besides, you have work to do. Go get the so-called Rogues that killed your wife." She yelped when he plunged the needle into her father's neck. His laughter rang through her small speakers as if he'd heard her. William spun around, clutching at his neck, as confusion set in.

"What did you do?" he shouted in alarm.

"My dear William, I have injected you with Rogue poison. I'm sorry but you're fired. Now the best thing for you to do is go out on your hunting mission like you were asked before until you turn, then hope like hell that it's your lovely children that are the ones to kill you."

"You have destroyed everything," her father whispered. Fear was clear in his hazel eyes. She bit her lip as she fought the oncoming flow of more tears. She and Thomas had killed him three years after the video date. They'd killed him because Nathanial had killed him first. Her chest constricted, and she wished desperately that she could destroy the monster all over again.

"No. Kathleen did. She didn't belong here, and she certainly didn't have business creating those abominations that you call children. I will finish this, and then I have my own plans for this world. The Fallen will all be destroyed, and humans will be meals again like they should be. We are their rulers."

Nathanial moved around to the other side of the bed, seeming to check Draven's vitals. He ignored William and said nothing else for several long minutes. The tape on the video was starting to go hazy, cutting in and out at times in flashes. She watched her father hesitate, touching the tender spot on his neck where he'd been stabbed with the needle, then clenched his fists furiously at his sides before he hung his head in defeat. She somehow felt the silent war that raged within him. He didn't want to waste what little time he had left to try and fight with Nathanial.

"Tell my kids I love them. Don't tell them I went on a suicide mission. That's not how I want to be remembered." His words were choked, as he struggled to form them through his growing tears. Nathanial gave a brief nod, and then waved his hand in a nonchalant manner.

Zarah remembered that night. It was the night after her mother's death. Her father had left for some time with instructions to stay in, taking Thomas with him for a short while. When her brother returned, he'd been Changed. But it was his return without their father that had concerned her.
"Where's Dad?"

"He called and said he has a mission to do. He won't be back for a while. It's just us now."

While she loved her brother, having just lost her mom, and then having her dad go off and disappear, it was a hard blow for a sixteen year old at the time. Nathanial showed later that night, shortly before dawn, to break the news that their father had went on a suicide mission to track every Rogue that could have been in the attack on Kathleen. He was out for vengeance—something that had always been strongly advised against in Guardian Code.

Now seeing the video, she saw that Nathanial had lied. Again. Her fists clenched hard, causing nails to dig into the palms of her hands and drawing a trail of blood. The dripping onto the hardwood floor below caught her attention, but she made no move to stop herself or clean it up. Her teeth clenched.

Nathanial looked back up to the camera and seemed to realize it was still on. He didn't care that the conversation had been recorded and continued to recite the vitals.

"Body temperature, ninety-five. Heart rate, twenty-three. The Change is almost complete." He'd stalked up to the camera to switch it off. Zarah was almost glad. She knew how painful it could be when the body made its changes. She was already nauseous seeing everything else. To watch him go through that as well would have probably been too much.

The heart stops, then restarts. During the restart, a new Vampire will experience multiple seizures for the first hour as the body adjusts to the new changes in the system. Though there's a heartbeat, they differ from a human's. They're lighter and much slower. They breathed still, but not with the need of having to so often. And their body temperatures ran much colder—usually around ninety-three or ninety-four degrees, while humans averaged at ninety-eight.

"Zarah."

Her attention was suddenly caught by Nathanial's whisper. He was close to the camera screen. So close that he blocked Draven's view. His mocking smile showed a hint of his once-dangerous fangs.

"If you're watching this, then I'm dead. That probably means you killed me too. I guess that's bad luck for you because you failed to ask for all of the information you could get I'm sure." He started, raising his eyebrows. His long, white-blonde hair hung around his face in wispy, stringy strands.

She held her breath with growing fury.

"Draven has a brother. His name is Seth. And their father is one of the Fallen Masters. It's possible that you're being hunted at this very moment. Now, does that interest you in the time you're watching this?" He smirked before the screen went black.

She sat in stunned silence, her eyes wide.

Seth?

Before she could think about it, she grabbed the device from the port on her computer and rushed from the room in a torrent of emotions.

Nine

She banged on the door with a violent force, the blood still dripping from her palms. She must have also cut her lip when biting it, because she tasted the metallic liquid at the corner of her mouth too. But none of that was important as she continued beating on the heavy frame in front of her. It took a few minutes before it swung open.

"Zarah? What are you doing? You should be in bed—" Seth stood before her confused, frowning. His round, gold eyes widened at her appearance.

"What the hell happened?" He almost shouted and reached toward her face. She jumped back with a fierce growl, baring her fangs. Her reaction clearly startled him as he yanked his hand away. She'd never realized how intimidating she could be for someone so tiny.

She charged and pushed into him without a word, continuing into his room. With the heel of her foot, she slammed the door behind them for privacy. He was pinned against the entryway wall and her forearm, despite that her head barely reached his shoulders and she had to crane her neck to look into his clearly baffled eyes.

"You have some talking to do." Her rage had erupted and she could barely contain the elemental power of her Fallen trait that wanted to burst out and burn him. Her free hand came up and flashed the memory stick to him as if it being presented would explain her own presence. It didn't. Seth still looked at her in concern and confusion.

"First, tell me what Unclaimed means."

She let him go and took a step back. If she could calm herself, maybe she could get the answers easier. Seth liked her. Or at least, Draven thought so. He had no reason to hide anything from her. But apparently he did. He had to know that Draven was his brother and their father was a Master that was bent on destroying them. Yet, he'd kept the information private.

Seth had been rubbing his bare chest, the spot where she'd held him, when she asked and froze. After a moment's hesitation, he looked down at the small memory stick again before taking a tentative step toward her.

"Does that have anything to do with Draven?"

She slowly nodded and blinked. A fan kicked on somewhere sending frosty air through the vents above them and sent little wisps of her long, auburn hair flying around her face. The silence seemed to stretch, but it gave her time to calm her turbulent emotions and become rational enough to talk to him. Seth's eyes met hers again. They'd grown dark and sorrowed.

"Let's get you cleaned up first, and then I'll tell you as much as I can for now."

She allowed him to reach forward that time and gently take her hand as he led her toward the nearby bathroom.

When she took a seat on the gray-marbled sink counter, a long silence stretched between them. He looked lost in thought, distant with a hint of a frown starting to crinkle around the corners of his mouth. She watched him begin to wet a cloth beneath the water. There wasn't really any need for medical or bandaging, she'd heal within the hour, but the dried blood on her hands and lip could use some washing away. Her injuries were already closing, looking like minor scratches.

Zarah caught a glimpse of herself in the mirror behind her. She looked disheveled and exhausted. Her skin was paler than usual with dark purple tones under her eyes. She'd been getting thinner due to feeding restrictions. The lack of sleep was evident all over. It was daytime, despite the closed shutters surrounding the building, and her body's natural need of sleep weighed heavy on her with each passing minute. With the current issue, she'd put her necessities on the backburner once again and rushed out. Taking a look over appearance, she almost snorted in disgust. There was a time when she cared more about how she looked. Now she sat there in a pair of old jogging shorts and a baggy gray shirt that hung half off her shoulder. She didn't realize until then either that she was barefoot. Her head hung down as she stared at her red-painted toenails on her dangling feet.

Seth's touch a moment later startled her and caused her to jump. She looked up to meet his apologetic smile and flushed. He stepped closer with the wet rag and began to gently clean away the blood from her lip without pulling his heavy gaze away from her. She swallowed the forming lump in her throat.

Seth was shirtless, standing close in front of her in only a pair of flannel pajama pants that loosely hung on his hips. Zarah wasn't blind. She would freely admit that the Fallen was very tempting, not just in looks, but in smell. Sugar cookies and vanilla…she inhaled sharply and took in the sweet scent that surrounded him.

As he moved onto her hands, she licked her lips and let out a sigh. She needed to break the silence.

"So…Unclaimed?" she asked, trying to bring the subject back up. He met her eyes again, showing no emotion.

"It's a term that means a Fallen was never accepted as any kind of Warrior. Not for the Masters, not for the Exiled. As a child, he or she was deemed unworthy. They are loners forever. They are never taught to fight or to use weapons. Cast out. Shunned. However you want to put it."

She paused. Nathanial had said Draven was Unclaimed. But as her partner now, she'd never know that he was considered weak at one time. He was the strong one between them. The level-headed one. And he could certainly hold a fight.

"So, Unclaimed are just abandoned entirely?"

"Yes. They usually never know they're of a Fallen bloodline and end up living the majority of their life as an average human. Their power might never develop or it gets stripped. Something like that."

He was skirting around the full explanation; she could tell. There was more to it—there had to be. If Draven could remember, he could tell the full story. She got lost in her thoughts until Seth began speaking again.

"You know something, don't you?" He had stopped, holding the rag gently over her hands. His were so large in comparison to hers, wrapping around them warily as he stared down questioningly. She swallowed and nodded.

"How much do you know, Zarah?" Seth's voice came out barely above a whisper, but she heard it clearly. He leaned in and her breath hitched again at his sweet scent. She backed away, her head bumping against the mirror. His touch was warm and she was tempted to reach up and tangle her fingers in his long, strawberry-blonde hair. Draven didn't seem to show interest in her anymore anyway. After the thought, she mentally slapped herself and bit her lip, turning her attention away from the Fallen. She loved Draven, and a small-forming crush on Seth wouldn't change that. Besides, there were much larger matters on hand than romance at the moment.

"I know enough," she managed to choke out. "What I want to really know is why you've been lying."

Seth stepped back and tossed the cloth in the sink with a sigh.

"Because I knew he didn't remember anything, and it was best kept secret. He is obviously in a much better place for him now anyway."

"So, you didn't show up that night as a favor for my mother. You showed up for him. Didn't you?"

She climbed down from the bathroom counter and stood in front of him. He smiled at her apologetically.

"No. That I was being honest about. Though, I admit, he did play into some of the reasoning for us staying."

Another silence stretched between them. She frowned in concentration. He stole a glance, eyeing her from head to toe, and she caught him. It caused her to blush and become suddenly self-aware of her wild appearance.

"What is on that memory stick, if you don't mind me asking?"

She was following him back into his apartment when he asked, and realized she still clutched it.

"Something I never want to see again."

Ten

"You're telling me that is a video of the night Draven was turned Vampire?"

Seth stared at her, his jaw slack, but his eyes grew dark with a deep fury. She'd settled on his couch, lounging back in exhaustion, and nodded.

"According to the little bit of information I gathered from it, Nathanial found him the night of my mother's murder in our yard and took him into the Compound." Her voice came out languid and her eyes began to droop. Despite the closed shutters around the building, her body's internal instincts knowing it was daylight had begun to take its toll.

"Why was he there?" Seth looked quizzical, but more like he was talking to himself.

"I don't know. I think he was trying to save her." She answered anyway.

Seth sat down next to her. She felt the nearness of his warm body. For some long ticking seconds, there was silence between them.

"How old are you?" she asked. The sudden subject change shook him momentarily, but he turned to her with a kind smile.

"Old enough, Sunshine. The Fallen come about differently than your kind."

"Tell me." He had her interest now. His laughter came tumbling out, and she caught herself staring at his lips.

"I will later. You look like you're about to fall asleep, and you most definitely need it. Can't have that light leaving those beautiful eyes." He patted her on the leg and made a move to get up. She blushed.

"Yeah, you're right. It's the daytime," she explained, though a yawn muddled her words. He smiled at her. She started to stand, only for him to gently push her back.

"Stay. You can sleep there. I don't have a problem with it, and it saves you from having to make the walk back to your room."

Zarah's brows furrowed in thought. It wouldn't kill her to sleep for a while on the couch there. She was already dead on her feet and could hardly move from the spot. Her eyes barely wanted to stay open.

With a sigh, she stretched out and handed him the memory stick.

"Watch this if you want, and wake me in a couple of hours." He nodded and turned away. Just as she closed her eyes again and began to drift into the darkness, she felt a blanket softly drape over her.

Ripping. Tearing. A flash of gray-black feathers. Blood dripping onto the white tile...

Zarah bucked when a hand touched her shoulder, her eyes popping open in surprise. It was only Seth staring down at her in concern, but her dreams had been in a different place and fear consumed her still as she continued to shake. The images from the video were still haunting her. She sucked in a shuddering, slow breath as her vision came into focus.

His hands were gently tucking strands of her hair behind her ear while he knelt down in front of the couch.

"Your wings...how are they possible?" she whispered when she could manage to find her voice. It was the first thing she could think of to say, and it was something she'd been curious of all along. Honestly, she'd always thought if they were real, the wings wouldn't be quite like they'd turned out to be. He frowned at her. Not out of annoyance, but as if lost in thought on how to best explain. He was clutching the memory stick, so she assumed he'd seen the video by then too.

"Only a full-blood has them. I know, they seem ridiculous and stereotypical." He gave her a lopsided, forced smile. "But they're a source of power, and a status symbol among our kind. If you have them, you're among our most powerful and elite."

She nodded in understanding, but made the mental note that Seth had somehow given away something. Draven had had wings.

"Okay, I get that. How do they work though? They're solid. Feathered. How do they go in and out of your back?" she asked incredulously.

He continued smiling and looked as if he were holding in laughter. Yeah, her questions came out a little silly, but they were genuine. She was truly curious.

"They grow."

"What?"

"Our shoulder blades...they have a special opening through our skin. When they're gone, it looks like two scratches. And they grow from there. Quite painful at times, honestly. That's why you don't see us walking around with our wings displayed very often or just popping them out for fun. Only when we're in battle."

"Wait," she started, beginning to sit up, squinting. "You're saying that they just *grow* out from your shoulders...like hair?"

"Exactly. It may look magical to someone watching, but it doesn't feel magical." Then he laughed. She stared at him in silence, not laughing with him.

He sighed and shook his head.

"You're really wanting to know what happened with Draven." He paused. It sounded like a statement, an accusation, rather than a question, but it was true. "You want to know why he just can't grow his wings back, especially now that you've shared your Fallen power with him?"

"Yes."

"Nathanial cut them off, that's why. When our wings aren't present, it's because we willed them away. We've no use for that grown set anymore, so the feathers fall apart and they leave us, but the main area at our shoulders remain the same for the growth next round. Draven went unconscious during a battle while his wings were still manifested, and what Nathanial did was cut them at the source. Then he turned him Vampire so that the area healed from the blood. It ended them entirely. Even now."

Zarah licked her lips and forced herself to swallow against her dry mouth. She could feel tears building again. "So, any Fallen can be turned Vampire?"

"Cut out our wings, the source of most of our power, and feed us the necessary blood, yes."

"I can't imagine how painful that must be," she only whispered, turning away.

Seth touched her chin, pulling her gaze back to him. His eyes were intense and bright, his face close to hers. She could smell the vanilla scent that hung in the air around him, and she fought the urge from lunging forward to have a taste. The thought gave her pause while she mused over whether or not a Vampire could feed from a full-blood Fallen, and if so, if anything happened. She shook her head in disbelief at the turn of her mind before focusing on him again.

"Actually, I feel sorrier for you," he whispered. His hand still lingered on her chin. It was warm and his fingers were slightly calloused from fighting.

"Why?" Zarah frowned, the confusion clear in the lines showing around her down-turned mouth.

"Because you're a warrior with a Fallen bloodline. And you don't have wings. You should."

Before Zarah could respond, he'd leaned forward and placed his lips on hers.

Eleven

Zarah had never been so shocked before. She also wasn't protesting to his kiss, and as he began to run his hand down her back and into a tangle of her long hair, she encouraged it by wrapping her arms around his neck. The kiss began to deepen and he was pushing her back against the couch with a sigh.

Of course, she'd kissed before. She'd done more than that. Despite her permanent nineteen-year-old age, she'd been around for a long time. This wasn't a new experience. But she also hadn't been looking for any kind of romance in recent months either.

Zarah closed her eyes as she enjoyed his tender touches over the sides of her legs and up her waist. Frighteningly, images began to flicker through her closed eyes. Draven on the table. His cut wings...bloodied and discarded.

Draven. Draven. Draven.

"No, no, no," she suddenly blurted, jerking away from Seth's touch and staring at him wide-eyed. "What are you doing?"

"I thought...you know...I thought we were enjoying ourselves here. I want you, Zarah. I've been wanting you," he said with a frown.

"I can't, Seth. This isn't right. You hardly know me. I don't know you very well. It's just not right." She didn't even know his likes or dislikes. Not like she did with Draven, who hated modern rap music—but loved classic pop—hated getting rained on, and loved sports cars and the color orange because it reminded him of a sun they couldn't be in.

"It's more than that, though, isn't it?" Seth interrupted her thoughts. He'd made his distance by pushing back on his heels and walked backwards until he sat on his bed several feet away. His eyes sent suspicious questions her way. She sighed.

"I love him. He is my Bond Mate."

"A Bond Mate that seems to disregard you now. I've noticed." His voice was flat and emotionless, but the words stung when they struck her. Anger swelled in her chest.

"Because of you!" She stood up with a shout, glaring.

"He thinks there's something going on between us," she continued as she wiped the back of her hand across her mouth to forget the kiss that just happened. It didn't matter. Her lips still tingled from their contact. He smirked at her. She scowled in return.

"Isn't there though?" he asked, standing now.

"No."

She couldn't believe the visit had taken these turn of events. Standing in the small apartment with Seth suddenly became too intimate. He towered over her, and she craned her neck up, looking defiant and determined.

"Too bad, Sunshine."

Zarah turned away and started to leave.

"Wait."

She stopped, her back still facing him, and held her breath. He came up behind her, too close, and reached around her waist. She swallowed, but when she looked down she saw he was handing her the memory stick back.

"I wouldn't tell Draven yet. Just a suggestion," he said as she took it from his grasp.

"Why not?"

"Because once he sees the video, the memories may come back. He's not ready to remember. There's a lot more to this than you know. Obviously, from the video you already know our father is not quite the friendly guy." Seth was bullying her into not telling? This seemed curious. She looked at him with suspicion.

"So, you do know more about that night than you let on?"

"Perhaps. I have to sort out some other things first. Not for you to know right now either."

She growled in response and stormed out with a slam of his door. More secrets. More questions.

Night had risen again she'd noticed, opening the shutters of the building.

Unfortunately, when she came stumbling into the hallway, furious still and with her wild appearance, she was face to face with Draven.

Twelve

Zarah stood silent and still, waiting for him to say something. She wanted him to say something to her. He stared at her expressionless, knowing the door she'd just stormed out of. Her mostly-dead heart thudded hard, slowly, in her chest.

"So..." he began, "...nothing is going on between you and Seth?" His voice was edged with an underlying anger. She licked her dried lips and watched his eyes scan her from head to toe. She was still barefoot and in the pajama wear from earlier in the morning when she'd first arrived at Seth's door. It was definitely not helping her case, and she mentally cursed Seth for not waking her earlier like she'd asked. Of course, he wasn't the only to blame. It was his couch she fell asleep on when she could've just used the last bit of energy she had to go back to her own room. It also would have saved her from that confusing kiss.

It was obvious he wasn't looking for an answer to the question. He'd already had his assumptions after seeing her. He didn't give her time to respond and started to turn away.

No. She wasn't going to let him walk off. Despite that she hadn't seen it, she kept imagining his injured Fallen body those years ago lying in her yard, later to be picked up by Nathanial. Maybe he'd sacrificed himself, or maybe he hadn't. Either way, he'd been stripped of his wings and turned Vampire because he'd been in her yard that night. He'd seen and heard the fight that killed her mother. If Draven hadn't already meant everything to her by then, he surely did now.

"No, Draven," she said quickly, her bare feet padding on the tiled floor while she ran to catch up. He continued walking, but slowed his pace.

"No? Then please, Zarah, explain. You just slipped out of Seth's room, right after dark, and you look like you've rolled out of bed." Each word sounded strained, growing more furious.

She sighed. They'd made some distance from Seth's apartment, and were in a different hallway. The Compound was silent besides them. His boots echoed, while her feet stomped in a rush to keep up. She reached out and put a hand on his arm, stopping him in the middle of the hall. He glared down at her in silence, his eyes dark and jaw set. She didn't remove her hand from his wrist.

"There's nothing going on. Will you stop? I fell asleep in there and Seth didn't wake me up. If you'd been paying attention, I was leaving the room angry." She left out the part of why she'd really been storming out for now. This probably wasn't a good time to bring that up.

Draven narrowed his eyes.

"Why were you in there in the first place though?"

Crap. Zarah hadn't thought this through. She hoped the casual slip of her other hand going behind her back to hide the tiny, black computer device wouldn't seem suspicious. Thankfully he didn't notice.

"I had questions to ask him about my mother," she quickly answered, thankful to pull the answer so fast from the top of her head. It was half-truth at least. He seemed to accept it and nodded.

A sly smile started to form and she reached up with one hand, playfully pinching one of his cheeks.

"You're jealous!"

"What? I am not," he huffed, trying to remain cool as he backed away from her pinching. She dropped her hand and pursed her lips.

"I was teasing. I know you're not. You don't care anymore." Her voice came out in a mumble, and she started to turn away to go back to her room. He came around in a flash to stand in front of her, his eyes showing surprise and hurt. She started to step back, but he stopped her by reaching out and placing both of his hands on her shoulders.

"I don't care? How could you think that?" The accent she admired came rolling out through each word. It was always more prevalent when he was emotional. She suddenly realized she had been trying to place Seth's voice. They had similar tones. It sounded Irish, but had a more ancient feel around the words.

Draven continued to stare at her, waiting for an answer. She stuttered in her thoughts and only gazed back into his eyes. The silver gleamed against the bright blue in his irises. She swallowed. He was shifting forward, his hands moving up to cup her face.

She felt her heart skip a single beat, and then her mind screamed.

No. She couldn't. As much as she loved him and wanted this, she couldn't. There was too much going on. She needed answers to the questions raging through her mind. They were at war, and there would be casualties. And she was keeping secrets from him.

Zarah didn't want to go into her bonding with Draven having secrets.

She didn't give him time to lean in and have their first kiss. Regret overwhelmed her when she pushed away. He looked confused.

"I can't," she stuttered. Her bare feet squeaked on the tiles as she rushed toward her room without looking back.

Thirteen

"Tonight, our world has suffered a great loss. Europe and its nations have been destroyed by air-bombings due to their aiding of Vampires. We have received military volunteers from several of the countries to join our Hunters. Any other countries or people caught aiding these monsters will be destroyed."

"Do you hear this shit?"

Thomas charged into her room. She'd been at the computer again with the video, skipping over the gruesome parts, trying to find anything she'd missed. In a rush, she closed out the screen before he could notice. The speakers in the hallway crackled the same announcement to anyone in the Compound that might've missed it on the television. He slammed her door and began pacing around her small space.

"Yeah. It seems things are worse, huh?" She turned around in her chair and faced him with a frown before taking the remote and switching off the never-ending news. She hated to admit she missed the bad reality shows.

"You're not kidding. Now whole countries are being bombed away just to destroy us." He sat down on the edge of her couch. A crease crossed his brows as he looked past her into the bedroom.

"Seriously, you can't make your bed at least on some occasions?"

Zarah huffed, blowing some of her hair out of her face.

"I make it when I want."

He let out a long sigh. She almost laughed at the lightening mood, but it was already turning dark again when he changed the subject.

"You look like hell, too."

She stood and shrugged, not meeting his gaze.

"I'm just tired of being locked up here. You know we should be out there fighting. Instead, we're inside like cowards."

"What good would it do for us to get executed though? Perhaps the Fallen are right on that point—" he started before she whipped around and cut him off with an angry growl.

"And since when do we let some Fallen control our system? The Compound is for the Guardians. Not them. They shouldn't get a say in whether we go out and fight or not."

He clenched his jaw. She saw the thought cross through his eyes but something else was there too.

"Many of you agree with them though, right?" she said with narrowed eyes, and crossed her arms over her chest.

"Yes. It's really for the best right now, Sis. You need to understand that. It would be suicide to go out there right now. We should arrange some sort of negotiation with the President, on neutral terms, for all of our safety. Either way, in the end, the result of this world isn't going to be pretty."

Zarah knew he was right. She hated when he was right. She sat back down with slumped shoulders, defeat clear in her features. The night was still early but exhaustion had already started to set in again.

"You're starving."

He hadn't said it as a question. It was clear in his voice. She looked back up at him and saw his worried frown.

"We're low on our supply. What do you expect? I'm sure I'm not the only one starting to starve." Maybe she'd sounded a little too quipped. She looked down in shame. Thomas came forward and knelt down in front of her, forcing her to meet his eyes again. How were they related? They didn't look anything alike. He had dirty-blonde hair and strong, chiseled features with large hazel-gold eyes; she had long, dark auburn hair with turquoise-violet eyes that were almond shaped and baby-faced features. Her lips were pouty and small, where his were narrow. His nose was large, but proportionate to his square-ish face, where hers was small and button-like and fit on her heart-shaped one. He was tall, at least six-two. She was short at around five-two or so. Thinking back to the video again, she saw so much of their father in him that she almost began to tear up.

"Didn't we just have a meeting about this though? To continue feeding from our supply like we always would until it does run out? Then we would figure it out from there? Yet, here you sit…starving…because you're refusing to take your own to allow everyone else the extra blood as long as possible."

His voice was soft, concerned. He reached up and ran his hand through her hair. She sighed.

"I've been under so much stress, Thomas. I have secrets and I can't tell them." Her words came tumbling out in a rush, tears with them. She went forward, and wrapped her arms around him in a tight hug. He started to form words; she could sense the questions coming.

Before he could get them out, screams began to pierce the outside air around The Compound building.

Fourteen

"What the hell is happening?"

Zarah and Thomas sprinted from her room and into the hallway where others had begun to meet up with confused and curious expressions. The screams continued somewhere outside. They sounded painful. She cringed each time one pierced the air.

"There are Hunters outside and they've snagged some Hiders."

She turned to see Draven walking into the crowd. He looked beyond furious, his fists clenched at his sides.

"Where?" she asked.

"On the north side of the building. I was coming out of the Lounge when I heard the commotion, and looked down from the balcony when I saw them."

She gave a short nod with gritted teeth before turning away. Her legs protested with each pounding step back to her room. Nails dug into her palms.

"What are you doing?"

She slipped bare feet into her combat boots and furiously grabbed her gun. Draven stood in the doorframe.

"I'm taking charge of the situation." She pushed past him and started down the hallway again, with him running behind her.

"You can't go out there! You're weak and outnumbered—"

"Weak?" She'd stopped, keeping her back to him. The anger was boiling in her system by now. What exactly could he mean by that?

"You know I don't mean it in that way," he started softly, reaching forward to touch her shoulder.

"I meant you're already under exhaustion. I feel it. I see it. If you go out there, you could get hurt. You won't be at your full strength."

She swallowed. Her hand gripped the gun at her side with force.

"Then don't let me go alone. Either way, I'm going."

She didn't look back to see if he went to get more weapons or the others as she took off running to the exit.

****

The rush of oncoming autumn air hit her face when Zarah made it outside. She took a deep breath. Scents of fire and ash filled her, and somewhere she smelled humans. Closing her eyes, she fought the immediate growing hunger. The desire to attack and feed overwhelmed her. The screams were back. She had to remain focused.

Slinking against The Compound wall, she remained hidden in the darkest shadows as she followed the sounds to the north side of the building where Draven had said he'd seen the Hunters. She only had her one gun, and she was still in just her shorts and baggy tee.

"Tell us where we can find more of you filthy bloodsuckers and we can end this easily."

She saw them. There were four Hunters surrounding two Hiders in a circle on the lawn. It wasn't much of a yard really, but it was space enough between the building and the road. There were a few stubby, wide trees, and concrete benches. A sign in front advertised The Compound to be a closed down hotel.

The Hiders were on the ground whimpering, injured from apparent burns and silver markings. She ground her teeth. Zarah knew she couldn't rush over yet. A plan had to be calculated first.

Her eyes scanned the group of Hunters one by one. All male. Most were. Hunters were employed by the President and other political leaders and consisted of the military, sometimes volunteers. Like it had once been her mission to protect humans, it was their mission to destroy vampires.

They were large. Not fat-sized large. But tall and muscled. Despite her supernatural speed, strength, and power, Draven could be right. She was outnumbered here.

"Well are you going to sit here and scream all night, or are you going to talk?"

One of the Hunters spoke again. His voice was rough. It sounded like sandpaper. Zarah followed his voice and glanced him over. He looked to be the elder one of the group. Perhaps in his mid-forties. Though his physical appearance was well-kept and it was obvious he was in shape.

"Come on, Boss, quit trying. Let's just finish them off already. They're not worth the time," another said impatiently. She frowned at the group, noting that they all seemed to be staring at "Boss" with frustration, their guns pointed at the vampire couple. He didn't have his drawn. He'd only been standing there trying to extract information. This made her curious of the middle-aged Hunter. Her feet edged a few more small steps away from the wall, still remaining in the shadows out of their view.

When the Hunters began to grab the vampires on the ground, Zarah froze. Their pained yelps filled the air around her and gave her chills. She watched in horror as three of the humans wrapped silver wire around the Hiders' necks in tight knots, throwing the other ends into a branch of a tree. They were going to hang them? That wouldn't kill a vampire, though it would be torturous. But then the thought occurred to her seconds later. No, the hanging wouldn't destroy them. The sun would.

The Hunters weren't going to wait a couple hours for the sun though. She saw one leave with a sprint, disappearing behind the fence, only to come back moments later with a gas can.

There wasn't any time left to lose. She had to go stop them.

As Zarah started toward the group with a low, angry growl, she realized she had company. Draven and Thomas had come outside sometime in the last few minutes to help. She almost smiled with relief, but there would be time for that later.

"What was that?" One of the Hunters asked, looking up and around the scenery after hearing them. She tip-toed behind him and tapped him on the shoulder. He whirled around, his eyes going wide at the sight of her.

"Hello."

"You're...you're a..." he stuttered.

"Vampire?" She smiled and revealed her extended fangs. The human smelled delicious. Before approaching, she had told the guys they were to try and not to kill them unless necessary. They'd agreed. It would draw less attention. They didn't want to attract more Hunters to the scene.

She flicked her eyes past the shocked human momentarily to see Draven and Thomas approaching the others. They were fighting. The one in front of her was still young, and apparently overwhelmed with his job. He started to fumble for his weapon. She threw her fist forward and connected it with his jaw, and it sent him sprawling backward across the grass. He stared up in horror.

"I don't want to hurt you. Actually, we don't want to hurt you or your friends. But you're hurting us. Do you understand?"

She knelt down by his side and took his shirt in her hands, bringing his body up. She aimed her gun at him.

"You're coming with us."

"Like hell," he said through a clenched jaw and threw up a leg. His foot landed hard into her side. She cried out in pain, falling on her back. Her vision swam. She heard him crawling toward her, and saw the flash of silver. The gun still remained in her hand by some odd chance. She was going to have to make the first move. The problem: if she fired her pistol, it could draw attention of other area Hunters. It didn't have the same sound as their larger rifles.

With some quick thinking and maneuvering, she turned in time and threw up her feet with a force before kicking out. They connected with the young man's head, followed by a sickening crunch, and his body crumpled on top of her. She breathed a sigh of relief at managing to get him unconscious instead.

After Zarah shoved the Hunter away, she slowly made it to her feet and looked around. The guys had managed to work together and get the others unconscious also. They were now at the tree cutting the Hiders loose.

"Are they okay?" she asked with a hoarse voice, limping over.

Draven nodded.

"They need blood to heal some of their wounds, but they'll be fine. They're coming in with us too."

She nodded and watched Thomas lead them gently inside. A few minutes later, other Guardians stepped out and began to drag the Hunters inside with them. Draven wrapped his arm around her waist to help her walk.

"Use one of them. To feed." He was whispering close to her ear, his lips pressed into her hair, as he referred to their new human captives. She looked up at him appalled at his suggestion, but inwardly found it appealing and tempting.

The last time she'd fed from a live human, she'd been Rogue. Could she do it again? Or would the memories be too haunting? What if somewhere deep inside, the Rogue virus still lived, and if she touched a live human she'd never be able to stop?

She only shrugged and let him continue to lead her back inside The Compound, not voicing her fears.

Fifteen

Zarah stepped into the holding cell where the humans had been tossed. It was more of a room than a cell. They had cots and a bathroom with a few small tables supplied with water and snacks. The only drawback: their feet had metal cuffs attached to chains drilled into the wall. They only had enough slack to get to the restroom when needed, and to lay down on their beds. Since their hands were free, she'd have to keep her distance when in there. Though at the time, she didn't have to worry much—they were still unconscious.

She thought back to Draven's suggestion and closed her eyes. They'd parted ways once back inside.

Feed. Feed. Feed. The voice teased her at the back of her mind. She bit her lip and dug her nails into her thighs. She didn't realize she had slid down the wall and was sitting on the floor until then. Before a decision was made, one of the Hunters started to groan, rolling over on his side in bed. He was waking up. It was the middle-aged man, the one they'd called Boss. He coughed. She smelled blood and her nostrils flared at the scent. The urge to sink her fangs into the man was powerful. Instead she let out a frustrated huff and cracked her neck, remaining in her seated position.

He heard her. Their eyes met. His gasp was audible but he stayed still. Her lips quirked into an amused smile and she sarcastically waved her fingers at him.

"You look so young."

Okay, she wasn't expecting that kind of comment. Please don't kill us, maybe. But a reference to how she looks?

"Well if you quit stereotyping, perhaps you wouldn't have a specific image in mind."

He stared at her in horror and shock. His mouth moved like a fish for a few seconds, trying to form words. She watched him, unblinking, with interest.

"I wasn't a part of that. I didn't want to be," he barely whispered. She still heard him.

"That's funny because I saw you out there when those two vampires were being hung to burn." Zarah could feel the center of her chest growing warm. It was a sign of the energy building. She quickly clamped it down.

"You have to be a Hunter now. Or you're under suspicion of being an ally of the vampires. I have too much going on in my family as it is. I can't afford the attention."

She narrowed her eyes. This human was chatty for a prisoner. Maybe he was telling the truth. She rolled her eyes, clasping her hands onto her knees. After a few seconds of awkward silence, he shifted, and she heard him moving on the cot. It got her attention and she turned back to him to see him sitting up. His bed was the closest to her. His ankle cuff was the only one that could come close enough to reaching her because it needed the slack from his side of the room to the restroom. If he even dared. She came prepared, taking a brief glance at the pistol sitting on the floor beside her, ready to be grabbed at a moment's notice.

The human saw her eye the gun and put his hands up in defense.

"I'm not going to do anything."

"Better not. I move fast."

He turned away, looking over his fellow unconscious partners before speaking again.

"Are you going to kill us?"

"It's not decided yet."

"You're not like the ones that are hunted." He spoke softly. His tone didn't hold any disgust or malice, but simple curiosity. She tilted her head to the side.

"As I said, since the war began, there have been stereotypes. All you humans do is cower behind them, rather than learn. We are not all evil. You all only know the silly myths that your kind created through books and movies."

She watched him swallow, sensed his nervousness.

"Even after all this, you sit there and say you might not kill us. I hardly believe you could be that kind though," he dared to snap back. She smiled and her fangs revealed in the dim light. He visibly flinched.

"True. But there are other things we could use you for." She stood, her joints cracking as she stretched, and slowly approached him. The gun was held in her hand down at her side. He didn't move from his position on the bed.

A silence passed between them while they stared at each other.

"I don't care," he said at last in a hushed whisper, though his voice trembled. He smelled different from other humans the closer she got. Blood had a faint metallic taste and scent to it. His smelled more earthly instead of metal. And sweet. Then again, she'd been drinking cold bags from blood banks for the last year. She didn't remember the tastes and scents much from her time of being Rogue, and before being rabid, she'd drank the bank bags then, too.

Shaking her head to clear it, she frowned.

"Is your name Boss?"

"Yes. Which is odd if you want to know the truth. I'm not suited to lead anything. Especially anything like what you saw outside."

Zarah had to admit it to herself. Boss seemed like a genuinely good human who just happened to be in a bad situation at the wrong time. The others she didn't know about. Thinking back to the events, they seemed to enjoy their job. She could see into her new guest's mind, a bit fuzzy in some areas, and knew he was being sincere about not wanting to be a part of it.

"What's your name? Or can I ask that?" He interrupted her thoughts.

Her eyes focused on him again, and she took another step toward his bed.

"Zarah."

He was scooting closer to the edge toward her, too. Good, she thought, it was exactly as she wanted.

"You do look young, now that I see you better."

"Yes. I was nineteen when I was fully fledged Vampire."

"How long ago was that?"

She shrugged, taking another tiny step forward.

"A while. Before you were born, I'm sure."

He let out a nervous laugh.

"I can't imagine you being older than me."

The others were still unconscious and Boss seemed to be relaxing more with each minute. He had a few purple bruises forming on his cheeks, but nothing serious. She watched him reach across to the little table nearby and grab a bottle of water.

"It's bad out there. I don't blame you and your friends for hiding out," he continued to talk. He wasn't really watching her anymore. She smirked. Already too trusting.

"I've heard. If you ask me, I'd rather be out there in the fight. At least letting humans know we can co-exist."

"How so? You drink blood. That much I do know is true about your myths. I don't know if a peaceful existence is ever possible."

She stopped. He was right in some ways. Humans and Vampires would never be able to peacefully co-exist. There would be times they could get along in some ways, but in the end, there would still be violence. Vampires would need sustenance, and the humans would stop going to blood banks in retaliation. She could see the outcome of that situation.

Boss turned and looked at her. He saw how close she'd approached by then but didn't move.

"Go ahead," he said with a sigh. He stuck out his arm toward her. She flinched in surprise. The scent was too powerful; she couldn't resist the urge anymore. With a flash, she stood beside him and had his wrist up to her mouth.

"There will be no harm to you," she said before she sunk her fangs into his soft flesh.

Sixteen

"He's what?"

Draven looked at Zarah incredulously. They all sat in the lounge some time later. And by all, it meant everyone, including the band of Fallen brothers. It was a bit claustrophobic. She stood in the doorway with her arms crossed, cheeks still slightly rosy from the short feeding.

"I said he's half Vampire. I'd say his daddy was a vamp, maybe left him when he was young, I don't know. Either way, he is. He just was never fully fledged and turned."

She was talking about Boss. The feeding had been brief. Not enough to even satisfy her, but it would suffice. She'd felt the guilt immediately afterward, then followed with the confusion because she'd tasted what he truly was. No wonder his scent had seemed so different to her.

"What about the others?" Draven asked.

"No, I think they're just your average human assholes. They were still unconscious when I left." She kept quiet about how she knew of Boss in the first place. As far as they were concerned, she only figured it out from his scent.

After a sideways glance at Draven, his eyebrows rose. He knew the truth though. She shook her head, warning him silently with her eyes, and turned back to the conversation. Thomas was saying something. She tried to focus.

"The Hiders are staying in one of the empty apartments down the hall. They're healing, but the man mentioned that there were a couple more in their residence when they were raided. They disappeared during the commotion."

"There's not much we can do about the separation. You know that. All we can do is hope the others made it somewhere else safely," Zarah said after a moment's thought.

"Where was the residence?" she added.

"He said it was only two blocks over from here."

"Let's go have a look tomorrow night, then."

Thomas and Draven nodded in agreement with her. Seth stood with a frown. She stared up at him in defiance.

"What?" she demanded.

"I thought we agreed it's best to stay inside. We don't need to go out into that war zone, and we certainly don't need to get involved." The other Fallen exiled warriors began to stand with him. Their large frames took command of the room as they tried to intimidate her and the others, but she wasn't going to step back. Instead, she stepped forward and growled. Her fangs glinted in the fluorescent lighting.

"No, that's what you agreed to do. We don't take orders from you. We will go out there and fight. You all can sit in here and cower behind these walls for all I care."

Her power came out with each word. By the time she finished, her hands emitted their violet aura and she felt the heat radiating through her chest. Seth took the first step back, his gold eyes dark and stormy with growing anger.

She turned on her heel without another word and stormed from The Lounge.

"So, are we going or what?"

She almost didn't hear Thomas running up behind her to catch up over the pounding in her head. Calming herself, she forced a small smile when she turned her head sideways to see not only her brother, but Draven and the other surviving Guardians some steps behind.

"Yes. Tomorrow night, we all meet at the garage doors at sundown. Make sure to have plenty of ammunition on you," she instructed.

"Oh, and Thomas? Bring Alyssa. I know she's going stir crazy, too."

She heard the boys whoop with joy as she proceeded down the hallway.

Zarah stopped at the apartment door where the two Hiders were staying and knocked. Thomas had talked with them earlier, but she wanted to check on them herself. The door opened, but she wasn't greeted right away. Instead, a figure moved immediately back into the room and left her standing inside the open doorframe.

"Hello," she said as friendly as she could.

"Hey," a rasp greeted her back.

She stepped inside and closed the door. The room was dimly lit, but she saw them both laying on the bed. Gauze wrapped around their hands, and bottles of blood sat on their nightstands. It was a young woman and man, probably newer Vampires. At least they were healing quickly.

"How are you feeling?" she asked.

"Better. We can't thank you all enough for saving us."

"No need." She shrugged her shoulders and took a seat in a nearby chair. Her legs crossed. She likely still looked like a crazy mess.

"I heard your residence was only a couple of blocks from here. Can you tell me some more information? Maybe about the attack, too?"

"Yeah…" the man began. He was lean and on the short side with short-cropped chestnut brown hair. His ears were slightly oversized for his head, along with his nose, but oddly, it didn't distort his appearance. His voice was what stood out: a deep baritone that really did not seem to match his small frame.

"…There were four of us originally. Every night, there are raids all over the city, the nation. We kept our home boarded to make it appear as if it was an abandoned house, and would make as little noise and light as possible. Apparently, they grew suspicious after walking our neighborhood a few times over the past week. They busted in and that's when they found us. We didn't have time to run. It was unexpected. We managed to break away for a few minutes on the walk toward the interrogation building, but that didn't work out so well. That's when you found us out front."

"And you said there were others at your residence?"

The female stared at her. She was quiet. Her eyes were dark, matching her light chocolate skin tone, and there were still burns on the side of her face healing.

"Yes," the male answered. He seemed to be the chatty one.

"There were two others, but they escaped during the commotion. Or at least that's what I'm guessing. They were there one minute, and the next, gone. The Hunters didn't see them. They only thought it was just us." He glanced sideways at the woman, touching her hand with gentle reassurance.

"Male? Female?" Zarah inquired of the missing Hiders.

"Both male. One of them was…strange. He'd only just arrived two days ago asking for a place to stay until he could get a more permanent residence elsewhere. The other was Cherise's nephew."

Zarah nodded in understanding, and met the eyes of the female, Cherise, again. There was worry there. But deep down, she saw something else. A warrior's strength and loyalty. It'd become personal to her now that the nephew was missing.

"Tell me, Cherise, were you or any of your family a Guardian once?"

The vampire swallowed. It was likely a struggle for her to speak still through the burn wounds, but she was fascinated by her. Hiders generally consisted of vampires who were created from humans, not born into the life. Sometimes in rare cases, Guardians who left the career and wanted to raise families without going out on missions every night for the bosses.

However, Zarah could always look at one and see it. The drive for the fight. The desire and passion and loyalty that comes with a natural warrior's blood. Just like what she saw in Cherise the moment she stepped into the room. The female was powerful, tall, and elegant—despite the burn marks that were healing. Her long, curly black hair was pulled back in a ponytail with a gold ring, and she lay on the bed wearing a white, sleeveless dress. It contrasted her milk chocolate skin. She even found herself admiring the exotic beauty. After a glance sideways, Zarah almost laughed out loud at the odd pairing, but she would never judge. It was apparent the male was very much in love with her and she was with him.

"Yes, my father was one of the first Guardians many years ago. He trained me as a child before I was fledged. I met Ray afterward though and decided not to join," Cherise interrupted her thoughts.

Zarah looked over at the male the same time she did. Ray looked down sheepishly.

"You turned him?"

"Yes."

She nodded and forced a smile. In a way, it was sweet. A happy love story for a couple. She sighed, thinking of her own dysfunctional love life.

After an awkward silence, she stood and began to head for the door.

"We're going tomorrow night to your residence. With some luck, your nephew and the other vampire would have stayed close enough in the area so that we can find them and bring them back here for temporary safe-keeping."

"Wait," Cherise started, standing from the bed. When she approached, Zarah saw how tall she was and stared up at her in awe.

"We'd like to come with you, please. This is our fight also. We want to join. And it's my nephew."

She nodded.

"Sure. Get rest tonight. Heal up. But I hope you both can do a better job than earlier with those Hunters."

Zarah walked out before another word passed.

Seventeen

The hallway was silent. It was a nice change, and after the bout of celebration earlier, Zarah welcomed the muted noise when she made her way down the winding corridors toward her room. There was something else nagging at the back of her mind though. It was too quiet.

She turned around and stared into The Lounge. Empty. Frowning, she made long strides toward the end of the hallway and pushed open the double doors of the gym. A few Fallen sat inside, cross-legged on the floor, talking amongst themselves.

"Hey. Where's everyone?"

One of them laughed.

"Probably in bed. It's been a restless couple of days." Cam said from across the floor. He smirked. She pursed her lips, her brows furrowing together in annoyance.

"Yeah, you're right. I don't know why I didn't think of that. I hadn't realized how late it was." As she replied, she heard the familiar sound of the automatic shutters closing on cue around the building's windows for the day. She sighed and began to turn back out of the gym with a half-hearted wave to Cam and his electric blue hair.

Halfway down the hall, she heard the doors whoosh open again and turned around on impulse.

"You should be sleeping."

Cam walked up beside her. She forced a smile at him.

"What makes you think that's not what I was about to do, and now you're interrupting?"

"Because I read into people well. It looks like you're not going anywhere near sleep for a while. Something bothering you?"

She shrugged one shoulder, turning into The Lounge and collapsing on a cushioned couch. He followed, taking a seat across from her. Zarah thought Cam was nice the few times she interacted with him, but could she trust him? Hell, she barely trusted Seth. Especially after the lies.

She narrowed her eyes at him in suspicion; his widened in return at her and he raised his hands in defense.

"I haven't done anything if that's what you're thinking."

"No. I'm just trying to see a family resemblance somewhere."

"What do you mean?"

"Are you all blood-related with Seth? He calls you brothers."

He laughed. It was a loud guffaw sound that made her outwardly cringe. Running his fingers through his shaggy wild-blue hair, he shook his head.

"No. No actual blood relation. Well, it's complicated really."

"How so?" she asked with a confused frown.

"Some of us are blood-born related, but as a whole, we're not all brothers. Do you understand what I'm saying?"

She gave a short nod.

"Yeah, I think so. Like Landon and Daniel are twin brothers. So they're definitely from the same family," she started. Her chin was in her hand with interest. He smiled and nodded in return.

"Exactly. Heath and I are brothers, too. Half. Same mother, different father."

"Oh really? You two look nothing alike. I'd never thought you were related."

He chuckled, leaning back and tucking his arms behind his head.

"So, what's the question?"

"Why do you call each other brothers?" she wondered.

"We are warriors, exiled, and banded together. Despite that we're not all blood-bound, we are brothers for eternity. We fight together always. There is never abandonment among us. One falls behind, and we all go back."

"Interesting."

Zarah let an awkward silence pass before she gave in.

"How are the Fallen Masters playing into our war?"

"You're a curious Vampire, you know that? Seth told me how you've been asking a lot about us recently."

She bit the inside of her cheek. The nerves began to bounce around in the pit of her stomach. Not only Seth had been talking about her to the other Fallen, but it was likely they wouldn't answer any of her questions either.

"I don't understand why he just doesn't tell you though. You're kind of important around here. You should have the knowledge at least," he added with a smirk. She smiled.

"He's told me a bit more. But that's me: curious. I'm always thinking of new questions."

Cam shrugged. "Not my business."

"So, you're not going to tell me anything at all, huh?"

"Oh, I'll tell you a few things. But you have to promise to go get sleep as soon as I'm finished. No rushing off to Draven or Thomas, or even Seth. Maybe...some of the information I give you isn't exactly information you should have yet."

Zarah stared at him in shock. His eyes were dark gold and serious. She sat up and leaned forward with curious anticipation.

"I promise," she whispered.

Eighteen

Cam had told her more than she'd thought he would. They'd sat in The Lounge late into the morning talking, mostly in whispers, until he finally pointed to the open doorway and told her to get to bed in a stern, but friendly command. That was when she'd started collapsing from daytime exhaustion. She knew he'd been right to push her out; she was going to need the sleep for later when her and the team were going to step out into the streets for the first time in days to fight.

"Many centuries ago, Fallen and humans interacted freely. Half breeds were normal. But when a Vampire male and a Fallen female bred a child, it caused chaos among the species. The half vampire-half fallen grew, and the father fledged him. It brought out much of the same kind of power you possess. It was frightening. The Halfling took advantage of it and held humans as slaves. It wasn't long before there were more from his own creation, whether from breeding or by forceful feeding. Our Masters began to seek them out, destroying them. A war was sparked one evening after two of the Masters' Warriors brutally murdered a Fallen's mate. She was a vampire. He vowed vengeance while they claimed ignorance, saying it was a mistake. They'd thought the vampire was one of the Halflings they were ordered to hunt. Many assumed they'd been set up by the Masters to spark the controversy. Either way, by this point, the Masters didn't care. They didn't even want the Fallen mating with Vampires for the risk of creating more abominations. The heartbroken and widowed Fallen exiled himself. He left everything behind, and as he traveled, began to meet others along the way who were starting to find themselves abandoned, destroyed by loss, or angry at the Masters for their ideas. That is the story of how the Exiled Ones came to be, how most of our feud with the vampires started so long ago. Though, as you can see, you won't find much of a problem being a vampire or Halfling amongst those that are Exiled. It's the Warriors you have to watch out for because of their commands to destroy you."

"Are you created from angels? Like Heaven?" she'd asked.

"It is said the first Fallen came to be from the mating of an angel and demon. Those beings are long extinct now. We just roam this earth as odd creatures with no real idea like vampires."

Cam had surprised her. The stories stunned her beyond words. They kept playing out over and over in her head as she curled up beneath her thick comforter in the bed. It was the first time she felt like she knew something other than half-truth, half-lie. She knew history. She felt it. An energy hummed somewhere deep inside her while she thought of the poor Exiled Fallen who'd lost his mate. The first Exiled One. She wondered who it'd been. She hadn't had the chance to ask the blue-haired guy before he shoved her from The Lounge with orders of getting sleep or else he was never going to tell her anything again. And she definitely wanted to learn more.

Zarah was dreaming again. She had to be. It was rare for a full-fledged to dream. But now she seemed to more often since her change. She remembered dreaming a lot as a child, though she didn't remember the dreams themselves too much. It'd been too many years.

But here she was, experiencing her third dream-like state in the last six months.

Fog encased her. She squinted. It was lifting slowly to reveal that she was inside a lighted tunnel. The end wasn't visible; it just stretched on endlessly in both directions as she spun around to find herself alone.

"Hello?" Her voice echoed loudly in the small space when she called out.

"Zarah."

She turned on her heel in a flash and faced the voice. He wasn't there a moment ago, but of course, this was a dream. He could appear when he pleased, how he pleased, and where he pleased. A thick lump formed at the base of her throat and tears threatened the corners of her eyes.

"Dad."

"Hey baby girl." His smile reached his eyes and he leaned forward to wrap her in a warm embrace. He and Thomas definitely shared a resemblance. Except her father had been a little older during his change, so he had more of the age appearance of a thirty year old.

"You still love me?" The question was blurted out in shock. She pulled away from him with wide eyes.

"Of course. Why would you ever think I don't?"

"I...we...killed you."

"Stop. Stop that right now." His voice grew stern. The tunnel faded away around her and they were suddenly standing on grass. She looked around, her mouth gaping at the sight of their old home. The house her and Thomas had to burn him in. The house where Mom died on the front lawn. She looked back at her father.

"You did what you had to do. I expected no less from you or your brother. I was Rogue; it was your duty. I couldn't live like that."

"But I could have saved you. Thomas—" she started. His fingers gripped her shoulders.

"No. I gave Thomas specific instructions. I told him the night I was injected what had happened. He knew. He knew all along that something was corrupt with Nathanial; he just didn't know exactly what was planned. By the time he'd figured it out, it was too late for him, too. That's why he turned you Rogue. He knew he had to start fixing the mess somehow."

* * *

"Thomas knew you were injected the night you disappeared, but he didn't tell me?"

"I told him not to. I wasn't even supposed to contact either of you. It was lucky that Nathanial didn't find out. I barely called in time before the poison set in."

"Why do you have me here?"

"Draven."

A wind from somewhere whistled around her and she stared at her father in confusion. This was suddenly reminding her of her mother's dream visit.

"What about him?" she asked in a suspicious whisper.

"Do you remember much from before your fledging? When you were still mostly human?"

She shook her head and swallowed. It was true. Small memories flashed on occasion: dress-up parties, studying on the couch for night tutoring at The Compound—which hadn't been offered for the last two decades because most children had went into home schooling instead thanks to the advancement of technology. She also remembered some training days, sparring with Thomas, as she learned kick boxing and martial arts. But most memories from so long ago, since the Change and the short time as Rogue, had grown fuzzy.

"There was a young man that visited on occasion to help me with my projects. Once in a while, he helped you answer some of your homework questions. He'd been homeless. But it was later I found out that he was an Unclaimed."

"You're talking about Draven? I've known him longer than I think?"

Her father nodded with a sad smile.

"I couldn't tell anyone who or what he was. Nathanial had met him once and grew suspicious just by looking at him."

"Why don't I remember?"

"It's been a long time. And you didn't see him much like I said. You were also Rogue at one time, honey. Coming out of that probably took a lot of your memory as it was."

"What happened that night? I saw the video. Mom directed me to it I guess you could say."

Her father became dreamy-eyed.

"I figured she would. That Kathleen is the most amazing woman I've met."

Zarah almost smiled. Even in death, he still showed his love and loyalty for her mother.

"It happened just as you found out. She was coming home from the store and she was ambushed. She'd been an Exiled One, but when the Masters discovered she'd mated with a Vampire, it didn't matter. They ordered her execution, hoping to prevent any Halfling anomalies. I was grateful they hadn't learned about you and your brother because you both were just inside the house and so close to the danger."

"So...Warriors destroyed her?"

"Yes."

"What was Draven's part?"

That's when she noticed his nervous swallow. He stepped back from her, turning his face toward the house with a distant gaze.

"Dad? What was it?" she repeated. Her voice began to sound hollow. She feared waking before she could find out the answer.

"He was there to save you from Seth."

Nineteen

Zarah awoke with a loud gasp, sitting straight up in her bed. It took her some minutes to adjust to the room. She had to focus after the dream, but the words still rang loudly in her head.

To save her from Seth? How? Why? She grabbed her pillow and stuffed it to her face to silence the frustrated scream. Just more questions needing more answers! With an angry huff, she flung the pillow across the room. It slammed into a hanging picture of a black cat she'd thought was cute. Unfortunately, the picture fell from its spot after being abused by the pillow, and the glass in the frame shattered across the wood floor. It only caused a string of swear words to leave her mouth before she obligingly climbed out of bed to clean it up.

The shutters beeped and buzzed when they opened. She'd grown used to them by now. Every morning at five-thirty: close. Every evening at seven-thirty: open. It was kind of nice, but growing more dangerous with each passing day. The Hunters outside would notice before long. They would need to move again soon. Probably back underground like before.

She took a glance outside after dressing and saw it was just as chaotic as it has been. Trucks lined the streets along the blocks and Hunters marched down sidewalks with guns at their sides. Some were dressed in military gear, others in regular street gear. Her intensified vision could see other weapons attached to belt loops—silver stakes and blow torches. Silver stakes? Her eyes almost rolled out of their sockets at the most horrible clichés. Still though, they were silver, and if stabbed through the heart or head, it would kill a vampire. Stabbed anywhere else, it would severely disable them. The poison could lead to death without treatment. It was torture for their kind.

Citizens were being ordered inside for the night with megaphones. Apparently there were nationwide curfews now. This could be an advantage for the team. At least now they may not have to worry about harming an innocent human during a mission.

"It gets worse every day that passes, huh?"

She jumped, startled, and whirled around away from the window. Draven stood in the doorway with his arms crossed over his chest, casually leaning against the frame. She hadn't heard him open it.

"I thought I locked that," she replied with a frown.

He shrugged and stepped inside.

"You did. But I know the code."

She gaped at him.

"What are you…stalking me now?"

He laughed and shook his head.

"No."

She couldn't help but return his smile anyway.

"Well, I guess you're lucky I was dressed before you barged in here then."

"Or maybe unlucky."

Her eyes darted to his and she began to stutter, trying to find a response. She didn't understand him lately. Sometimes warm and so close, but other times distant and cold.

"Sorry, that was inappropriate," he said after an awkward silence.

"We're all ready when you are. Full dark is almost here. Do you think it's best to go on foot?" He quickly changed the subject. She looked toward the window again.

"Yes. That's the best plan. We can't take vehicles anymore. They have too many stop points and checks. And now citizens have a curfew."

Draven nodded in understanding and began to head back toward the door. He stopped about halfway across the room and turned to face her. His expression was different; he looked like he was thinking hard about something with his lips pressed into a thin, concentrated line, and his narrowed bright blue-gold eyes. She stared back.

"What is it?" she asked, nervous under his gaze.

Without warning, he was in front of her. He surprised her when his hands wrapped tightly around her waist and pulled her against his body. The rich, cherry aroma that was a part of his scent intensified. She felt her heart swell when his tender lips touch hers, and within seconds an involuntary moan escaped. It caused his hands to snake their way up into her hair, and her hands to wind around his neck in hopes of never having to let go of the moment.

He nipped at her bottom lip. Their fangs bumped into each other. They both let out short laughs and pulled apart, but remained intertwined with their foreheads touching.

"I had to do that before we went out there. Now if I die, I can die happy."

She smiled.

"We're Bond Mates, remember? You die, I die. But that's not going to happen. So let's go kick some ass."

Twenty

"You go ahead, I'll be at the doors in a minute," Zarah said when she and Draven stepped from her room and into the hallway. He glanced at her questioningly and she flashed a reassuring smile before turning to walk in the opposite direction.

She wore casual dark skinny jeans and a black tucked in long-sleeved V-neck cotton shirt. Her waist was weighed down by a leather gun holster, holding two handguns and a large, silver dagger. She'd pulled her long hair up into a messy bun, and as always had on her favorite boots.

Before leaving, Zarah had something she wanted to do.

"Aren't you supposed to be going out on your little mission?" Seth mocked, standing in the doorway of his apartment after she'd knocked. She pursed her lips in thought and nodded.

"Yeah. I had to stop by and tell you something first though."

"Oh yeah? What's that? You change your mind since kissing Draven?"

Zarah froze. He must've seen the shock across her features because he laughed.

"I told you, I can read emotions and thoughts. Not too well from you, but when it's projected intensely, I can faintly pick it up."

"Oh. Right," she started, fumbling for words. Her feet shuffled nervously. She thought of the dream and took a tiny step backward. Seth frowned down at her.

"But no, that's not it," she added.

Seth blinked at her, waiting patiently.

"I came to tell you that I talked to my father. He told me things. He told me..." She couldn't finish and shook her head, glaring at her feet.

"I'm going to tell Draven the truth tonight about his history. He needs to know. That's it."

Zarah tried to turn away quickly, to leave before he could say anything or to protest, but she hadn't made a step before his arm lashed out and took a grip around her wrist to pull her back.

"Your father told you what?" he demanded in a low voice.

"Don't worry about it."

She struggled against his grip to no avail.

"Let me go," she growled.

"Tell me and I will."

"Let's just say that next time you want to attempt to murder me, you better make it a fair fight." Her words came out through clenched teeth as she flashed her fangs and bright, angry eyes up at him. His hand dropped her arm in surprise and she turned, running down the hall toward the entrance without another word.

They were all ready and waiting for her when she arrived. Draven looked at her questioningly but she turned her gaze away in shame. Thomas stood by Alyssa holding her hand. They smiled at her.

"Hey, Alyssa, glad you could come." Zarah approached and wrapped her arms around the blonde vampire in a warm embrace. She really needed to bond more with her. After all, they were technically sisters now that her brother had committed. He'd made his official Bonding Pact the night after she'd cured him. It cured Alyssa. Now her red eyes were gone, replaced by their once beautiful emerald green and sparks of bronze.

"Of course. I wouldn't miss the opportunity of a fight," Alyssa replied with a playful smirk, winking. Zarah laughed and pulled back, looking over the others. Cherise and Ray were among them. They hung to the back of the crowd of heavily-armed Guardians. She pushed through the buzzing crowd toward them.

"Are you sure you don't want to stay here? I promise if we find your nephew, he will come back with us," she asked Cherise. The exotic vampire's dark gaze met hers. Both Hiders had healed overnight.

"I'm sure about this. I trust you and your group, but we want to go. Keenan may not trust you," she answered. Zarah nodded in understanding. She noticed the two had been provided casual clothes—pants and plain black shirts—with holsters and weapons around their waists. It was a relief and she only hoped they would be able to defend themselves well if a situation arose.

Zarah let out a quick whistle to get everyone's attention before motioning to the door. They'd discussed a brief plan before about the mission, but she knew it wasn't well thought-out. Cherise and Ray would lead them along the darkest route to their raided home, and from there, they'd have to do a ground search without being seen by the Hunters. Simple enough. She hoped.

The Fallen weren't going. She could be thankful for that. After the dream and confrontation with Seth, she didn't want to look at them for a few hours at least. It was bad enough living under the same roof. She wasn't sure if Seth had been trying to kill her that night, but it seemed that's what her father had been trying to say. It hurt to think about that kind of betrayal. But there was no time to sit around and demand answers to never-ending questions. Cam provided a few at least.

As she watched everyone proceed out the doors with quiet grace, she caught sight of Draven again. He was definitely going to find out the truth. He needed it.

He seemed to sense her stare and glanced sideways at her.

"Are you okay?" His voice came out in a worried whisper. They were behind most of group, Thomas and Alyssa in front of them, Cherise and Ray holding up the end of the line, and were outside. The frosty air stung her face. They skimmed along the wall of the building, keeping their eyes on the surroundings and guns drawn and ready if needed.

"I'm fine," Zarah whispered back. After that, the group remained silent, careful.

Trucks rumbled by in the street. Hunters stomped along the sidewalk several yards away looking for signs of movement. Anytime one passed, the group became still until the area was clear again for another few minutes.

After an agonizing, tense, hour of walking, stopping, walking, they'd arrived on the street of the Hiders' residence. The gasps behind her said something wasn't right. She looked back at Cherise briefly to see horror etched in her normally calm features before following her gaze to the end of the road at a lot where a house once stood.

She'd imagined it used to be beautiful.

But now it sat in ruins—charred and ash.

Twenty One

Debris crunched under Zarah's feet while they explored the ruins of the old home. She kept glancing over her shoulder for any sign of other movement. Draven stayed close by, his gun at his side. It had taken some time to calm Cherise down enough to get to the destroyed house. Ray walked with her around the perimeter some distance away as they called her nephew's name in hissing whispers toward the cluster of trees at the property line. Zarah's sympathy sparked.

"I don't think Keenan or the other one is here," she muttered to Draven.

He started to say something but was interrupted when shouts came from the road. They all turned in the direction to see a group of Hunters running their way.

"Oh hell," Thomas growled.

"What do we do?" Jerry asked, standing on top of a charred wooden beam a few feet away. His silver eyes flashed with the anticipation of an oncoming fight.

Zarah looked around at her group. With the exception of Cherise and Ray, she knew they were all different. They'd all changed into something new in the last few months thanks to her blood. She was surprised the two Hiders hadn't noted their unusual differences.

The Hunters were yelling at them to drop their weapons and aiming large guns at them. They wore heavy masks to cover their faces and military camouflage. These weren't volunteer hunters. They'd been commissioned to the task by the nation's leader to eradicate the vampire species and control the new order of the country.

"We fight," Zarah replied with a throaty rumble. She took a fierce stance and withdrew both of her pistols. The others followed suit. She caught some of them smiling, ready.

"By the order of the President, you are to surrender!" One of the Hunters shouted. They'd stopped at what had once been the house entrance, and it'd become a staring contest between all of them.

"We will not harm you unless we have to, humans. We would like to arrange a peaceful negotiation with your president." Zarah did the speaking. She tried to keep her voice calm.

"It's not going to happen, monster," another Hunter spat. Zarah clenched her jaw, but refrained from attacking until necessary.

One of the Guardians moved, causing busted concrete to shift and tumble. A Hunter started to direct his gun in the direction of the movement. Before something could be done to stop them from firing onto the group, there was a blinding flash and two Hunters gasped. Blood flowed from their throats, shots rang out, and the group ducked to avoid being hit. Zarah looked around in confusion. Cherise screamed.

Another flash and the last two hunters fell in a bloody heap with their partners. The metallic-sweet scent of the humans' blood permeated the air around them. Zarah felt her fangs extend in brief excitement before she turned to Draven with a frown.

"What the hell just happened?"

He shrugged and began counting the group members. No one had moved from their spots, but now they had four dead Hunters on the sidewalk in front of them.

A throat cleared nearby, which quickly grabbed their attention again. A chorus of safety switches clicked off from the weapons and pointed in the direction of the noise. Zarah's eyes widened at the sight that greeted her.

"I just figured you could use a little help. You're welcome."

Ethan stood at the corner of the burned home with a smirk and hands raised in defense, blood still at one corner of his mouth.

Thomas let out a string of curses behind her.

"Now, Thomas, that's completely uncalled for. Such tacky language." He tsked.

"Tell me why I shouldn't shoot you," Zarah said, aiming her gun at the vampire. Ethan used to be Rogue. In fact, he was the first Rogue that cured since her—after forcefully taking her blood during her captivity a few months ago. He was also the one who had initially turned her brother Rogue, and the first intelligent one—with thanks to another of Nathanial's experiments because of Thomas' blood.

"You shouldn't shoot me because I'm one of you now, and because I just saved your ass. Right?" He cut through her thoughts. She felt the heat rise.

"You all know each other?" Cherise suddenly asked as she interrupted the conversation. Zarah hadn't heard her approach, and turned to face the woman with clear surprise.

"What do you mean?"

"He's the other Hider that was staying with us." She took a second to offer a sad smile to Ethan.

Zarah blinked. She could not be serious. After an awkward silence though, she saw it wasn't a joke and let out a frustrated sigh. When she holstered her weapons, Thomas let out a gasp.

"Sis, you can't be serious? Shoot him or I will!"

"No. He's coming with us...unfortunately. I'll discuss it with you later. For now, this is the decision." Her words weren't enthusiastic at all, and her eyes remained on Ethan. His smile grew when she spoke, which made her frown and disgust deepen.

"It's best you stay on my good side, or I will shoot either way," she warned Ethan darkly. He quickly nodded with a mock salute.

"Keenan?" Cherise asked with worry. Her attention was nowhere in particular, but Zarah assumed she was asking the new vampire.

"I'm sorry, Cherise. I haven't seen him. We ran out of the house together that night and were separated when we went into the woods. I figured he'd stay close, but there's been no sign or smell anywhere."

Cherise nodded and slumped her shoulders.

"We should go. I think I hear more trucks," Draven whispered near Zarah's ear. She jumped at his touch, a small shiver tracing down her back, before agreeing.

She turned to Cherise. Words couldn't form. How could she explain that they would not be continuing the search for the nephew until another night.

Thankfully she didn't need to. Their eyes met and tears formed in her eyes as she silently understood what Zarah was about to tell her.

"It's fine. I understand that we should be getting back. Thank you anyway," Cherise whispered. She nodded and watched Ray lead her toward the back with his arms wrapped around her shoulders in comfort.

"Ethan, you're in the back with us," Zarah instructed, using her gun to motion him toward where her and Draven stood. He shrugged and approached them.

"Do you have any weapons on you?" Draven eyed him suspiciously.

"Only these." Ethan flashed his fangs with a charming smile. Zarah rolled her eyes. Thomas and Alyssa stepped over fallen glass to them. The others began to descend the broken, burned house as they started back to The Compound.

"You have blood on your lip," Thomas sneered in disgust. He took Alyssa's hand and they walked away. Zarah sighed. She planned to talk to him when they were back. Ethan used the sleeve of his jacket to wipe away the red drops.

Zarah kept her focus on him, unblinking, the entire trek back. Ethan was going to be a problem. Her gut screamed at her how wrong this was to have him there. At the same time, she hoped she could use his presence as an advantage.

Twenty Two

"Are you out of your mind?"

Thomas was in a near shout, his fangs extended in anger. Zarah stood in the middle of her room calmly staring at him, quiet while he paced and yelled.

When he stopped in front of her, his eyes blazed dark. She didn't blame him for being mad. Ethan was situated down the hall in his own room, and worse, it happened to be next door to her brother. It was the only empty one left though without having to move and rearrange others.

"We didn't have much of a choice," she started.

"Oh, I think I could have easily shot him and taken care of that dilemma," he interrupted. She sighed and rolled her eyes.

"Look, I know it's Ethan. I know he was the one that turned you Rogue and helped Nathanial. But maybe there's something else there. Maybe he can help somehow. I don't know. He could have killed me that night, but he didn't," she continued with a shrug.

"If he lays a hand on you again, I will kill him."

She smiled.

"Not if I do it first."

After Thomas left, Zarah took a shower. Her thoughts were muddled. Draven. Seth. The world in general. It was all hell.

She needed to visit the captive Hunters. Dawn was approaching, but time didn't matter to her anymore. Sleep was becoming a privilege. Her body had become constantly exhausted and starved. Since she'd last fed on Boss, she'd decided that she wouldn't do it again.

On her way down the hall, Draven walked up beside her. She almost sighed out loud, knowing the coming dreaded talk with him. It was being postponed as long as possible.

"Where are you headed?" he asked casually, breaking into her thoughts.

"To visit the Hunters. We need to figure out what to do with them."

"Have you had anything to drink since the other night?"

She stopped. He halted his steps with her and their eyes met.

"I'm not doing that again," she whispered, her eyes darting around with paranoia.

"You need to do something. And don't feel guilty about anything either. You're a vampire. It's in our nature. It's not like you're lost to the bloodlust, so it'll be fine."

"Have you been feeding from them?" she asked with narrowed, suspicious eyes. Her weight shifted to one foot and a hand went to her hip. He shook his head.

"No, but one or two others have. I'm not naming names. Don't worry, there's not any harm coming to them otherwise. They're being taken well care of."

She thought for a few minutes before nodding slowly. Her worry for the Hunters mostly stayed with Boss. As if sensing it, Draven placed a hand on her shoulder.

"Boss is fine. What's so fascinating about him though?"

"I don't know. I just feel a strange connection." Her voice was hoarse and tired. She shrugged and looked toward the direction of the room where the humans were kept.

"I'll see you later," she added before stepping away from him.

*****

The room was mostly dark when she entered with the exception of the two small lamps. A soft yellow light emitted from the bulbs, casting an eerie glow. When she unlocked and pulled the heavy door open, entering, the humans stood from their beds in alarm. Well, the other humans. Boss remain seated on his. Calm and collected. He even smiled at her. She returned with a small smile at him.

The other three males were on edge. Zarah was glad to be at a distance away from them, and even more thankful for their chained feet. She met the eyes of the man she'd fought with briefly. He was young, no older than twenty, but hate already filled his cold gray eyes.

"Heard you went on a little trip through town tonight. Run into any of our friends?" The young Hunter mocked with raised eyebrows.

"Matter of fact, we did. They're dead." She flashed a smile, revealing her fangs, and leaned back against the door with her arms crossed over her chest. She'd walked in barefoot again, only in a pair of lime green silk pajama pants and a black tank top. Her hair was still wet from the shower.

"You little bitch—" He started toward her furiously, only to be stopped by the end of the chain. His fists clenched at his sides.

She rolled her eyes.

"Relax. No one in my team did it. You need to learn we're not all evil monsters." And that was the truth. No one in the team had killed the Hunters. Ethan had, and he certainly wasn't part of the Guardians.

"If you're not, then why are we being held here?" Another asked. He didn't sound angry, just curious.

"We're sick of the violence," she hissed. "Would you rather us kill you instead?"

"It depends on what you plan on doing to us. We don't want to be used as blood donors."

She flinched and shook her head.

"Mostly, we want to know if one of you can help us contact your president. We want to work out negotiations hopefully to end all of this. A peace. Explanations. Understandings."

Boss and two of the Hunters nodded, not seeming to have any problems with the arrangement. The young man at the back continued to glare daggers at her.

"Have a problem?" she directed at him.

"You're still a monster. I don't care how pretty you appear to be on the outside. You're a walking nightmare that should be destroyed."

Zarah stared at him unblinking for a long awkward silence before stepping forward. She moved to the middle of the room, risking herself around the men, knowing she was unarmed. She had her own defense.

When she was face to face with him, she smirked. He sat down on his cot with his eyes on hers in a strange trance. She felt the growing heat in the center of her chest. The white-violet heat building through her fingertips. She leaned forward until her face was only inches from his and flashed her fangs.

"I can be your nightmare."

With that, purple flames erupted from her fingertips as she wiggled them at him with a smile. The others gasped in surprise.

"Zarah!"

She spun around, the flames extinguishing immediately, to see Seth in the doorway staring incredulously at her. Fury was written in his features with trembling fists at his sides.

Twenty Three

Zarah ran out of the room. Her ears were ringing, and vision blurred. She'd barely pushed by Seth. He grabbed her arm, stopping her, as she tried to rush down the hall.

"What the hell was that back there?"

She tried pulling away from his grip but he held firm. Her head and hands shook until she finally slumped her shoulders in defeat.

"I don't know. I was so angry. He struck my last nerve. And I'm just really tired and thirsty. I don't know…" she kept stuttering, looking everywhere but at him.

He touched her face and pulled it around tenderly to meet his eyes. They'd lost their anger. The gold irises lightened with concern.

"You're so unusual, it's dangerous. This army you're building is all fine and dandy. My brothers and I are okay with that. You need backup and we understand. But with the state of the world, if you get caught by one of the humans or by one of the Fallen Masters, it could be a much bigger problem. And now at least four humans know how different you really are from other vampires. This can't be good."

"Well...perhaps you should have ended my life that night after all. It would have saved a whole world of trouble." She tried to pull away again, but he still held tight.

"What did your father tell in that dream exactly?" His voice came out in a dark whisper and he leaned down close to her face. "Because I was never there to kill you."

She stopped and looked at him through wide eyes.

"He just said that Draven was there that night to save me from you. What did he mean by that other than the possibility of you attempting to destroy me while the Warriors outside shredded my mother apart?"

Seth stepped back and dropped her arm. It was enough to give her the space she needed to leave him. He remained silent. It was plenty to tell her that he was hiding something. Maybe he'd been there to kill her, maybe not. Either way, he wasn't denying it and he wasn't confessing. Another spark of anger flared in her chest.

"Stay away from me," she growled and started to turn on her bare heels. His eyes trained on something behind her with amusement, and when she turned, she saw Draven standing there with a confused frown. She froze in horror.

"What's going on here?" he asked. She sensed his growing puzzlement to the situation. Seth stood protectively close behind her, and her emotions raged wildly through anger and hurt that she knew he could sense from their bond. Words tried to form, but she couldn't bring herself to speak. She looked between the two guys nervously. Her eyes stopped on Seth's slow-forming mischievous smirk. He wouldn't dare, she thought furiously.

"We were discussing the hot kiss that happened the other night in my room. I told her I don't like to share, but it's obvious she likes to go jumping around indecisively." His hand waved nonchalantly toward Draven. Zarah's jaw dropped in shock. He'd went too far.

"Is that true? Did you two kiss?" Draven asked when she spun back around to face him.

"I...yes...but I can explain," she started, stuttering. She tried to step forward, reaching out. He pulled away from her. His face showed clear disgust; his lip curled up in rage.

"No need. I should've known there were other reasons to you being in his room. I've sensed strange feelings coming from you the last week."

"I'll see you later, Sunshine," Seth cut in with a smug smile before he turned and walked away. She barely glanced over her shoulder. How had it taken this turn of events? When she turned back to Draven, he was walking away too, and she rushed to catch up.

"Draven, wait. Please, let me just talk to you."

He continued to ignore her. She watched his muscular frame move gracefully through the hall in front of her. He wore a plain black tee and a pair of a gray sweat pants. It'd been obvious he had been about to go to bed for the day before finding her in the hall. The shutters were closing. She caught a glimpse of the lightening sky as they slowly wound their way around the windows.

"Please," she pleaded. She couldn't remember the last time she'd sounded so young and vulnerable, but the thought of losing him hurt. It cut into her like silver, and she could feel the pain splicing into her cold veins. He must have heard it in her voice, or maybe he felt it too, because he stopped at his door. His back remained facing her as he waited for her to continue speaking.

She swallowed the lump in her throat and stepped closer.

"I didn't. I didn't kiss him. He kissed me. And that's why I left so mad. But that's not why I was there. I've been keeping secrets from you, and I'm sorry, but I want you to know—"

Her words were cut off by a blast downstairs.

Twenty Four

Hunters raided the building. They'd waited until the morning daylight hours to ambush them, which Zarah had to admit was a good idea. It was what she would have done. To attack at an enemy's weakest moment.

She never finished her talk with Draven. Instead, it was cut short with the blast of the downstairs door blowing away from its hinges, followed by shouts and gunshots. The Guardians came rushing from their rooms armed and prepared for the coming fight—Zarah and Draven stared into each other's eyes for long, silent seconds as if time stood still. They read into each other. She feared this was going to be her last time seeing him for a long time, and she wanted to memorize every detail of his face.

He had a dimple on one of his cheeks. Every time he smiled, it deepened. The gold flecks in his eyes were different sizes and shapes, but the blue irises surrounding them were what she loved most. They changed color with his emotions—dark navy when he was angry or frustrated, bright cerulean when he was passionate or joyful.

She imagined he was taking the time to do the same thing with her. He slowly moved forward and brushed a hand across her face. The chaos began to rush onto their floor as the Hunters ran up. The Fallen walked into the hallway with their swords ready to join the battle. Everything began to blur around Zarah.

"We only want the girl, the leader here," one of the humans called out above the noise. Silence seemed to pass and eyes landed on her. She ignored them and stood on her toes to place a gentle kiss on Draven's lips. He looked at her in confusion.

"There's a memory stick in my bedroom by the computer. Get it. Watch it. Try to remember," she whispered in a rush. He tried to pull her back when she started to step away with a sad smile.

"No, you can't go with them," he growled.

"It'll be fine. If I go willingly, they'll leave you all alone. I can see it in their minds."

"I don't give a damn."

"I love you." A tear trickled down her cheek and she pulled herself away. It was the first time she'd voiced her feelings. She watched the flood of emotion wash over his features, but never gave him time to say anything back before she walked away.

A few of the Hunters had found the captives and released them. Boss stood off to the side, a grim frown creasing his face, as she crossed the floor toward the waiting humans.

"You know I can't go out in daylight," she quipped. "And you have to leave everyone else here in peace if I'm to go with you quietly."

"Yes, those are our orders. We're only here for you on behalf of the President. We have a transport vehicle in the garage that is safe for you to travel in during the daylight," the Hunter in front answered. He kept his weapon trained on her; she continued walking forward with her arms raised. Her comrades stood along the walls defenseless and nervous, watching her. There were too many Hunters for them to fight. She knew this had to be done to save them all. She briefly met Seth's eyes before turning away again. Her head held high in determination, despite the confusion. How had the President found out any information about her specifically? And why did he want her alive? Something was unusual about this situation and it didn't sit right in her gut.

The young Hunter she'd threatened earlier stood near the group she approached. He was smirking, smug and thrilled at her capture. She narrowed her eyes at him and imagined the day that she'd get to bite into his neck. As if sensing her thirsty desire, his smirk disappeared and his eyes averted elsewhere. Zarah smiled.

When she was close enough to the groups' leader, she tilted her head in curiosity. He wore a cloth mask that covered most of his face, but his bright green eyes were visible beneath the metal helmet. She smelled him.

"What is your name, Sir?"

"Does it matter?" He didn't sound harsh; he sounded anxious.

She shrugged.

"Might be nice to know a name if I have to travel with you. That's all I'm asking."

"Zeke," he answered after an awkward silence.

Zarah nodded with a soft smile.

"Well, what are we waiting for? Let's go."

She started forward. A few more humans surrounded her in a threatening circle. She didn't hide her fear of their new, larger guns while she stood in the center unarmed.

Zeke raised a set of silver cuffs.

"Sorry, but it's precautionary," he said when he stepped forward and slapped them onto her wrists. She hissed in pain at the already setting silver poison. Somewhere in the background she heard Draven scrambling to get through the crowd.

"Stop!" she yelled backward though she couldn't really see. Her eyes sought the front of the crowd as she started to get escorted out. They landed on Thomas and Alyssa, where she saw Alyssa struggling to keep a grip on her brother.

"Thomas, Thomas…" she stuttered quickly, forcing her captor to stop in front of the pair when she planted her bare feet firmly to keep from moving further.

"Let me hug my brother!" she growled at the Hunter. He at least allowed her the opportunity and stepped back. Thomas scooped her into a tight embrace. She couldn't wrap her arms around him because of the cuffs, but she used the chance to say what she needed to as quick as possible.

"There's a memory stick in my room. I've told Draven to find it and watch it. Tell him I've told you to see it too. Help him...and don't worry about me. I've figured it out."

"Okay, come on now, it's time to go," Zeke's gruff voice came behind her. He pulled her away from her brother's grasp and she smiled. Thomas looked at her in confusion. She only nodded and wiggled her fingers at an attempted wave. Zarah took a last look back over her shoulder. Seth stared at her, his eyes dark and dangerous.

"So how did the lovely President hear about little bitty me anyway?" she asked when they all arrived in the garage. A few Hunters stayed behind in The Compound to keep guard over the others while these took her away to wherever they were going to go. Zarah already knew that the humans left weren't going to survive much longer, and the ones traveling with her then knew that, too.

There were two sport utility vehicles with daylight blocking tint wrapped around all of the windows. A thin, protective cloak was still placed over her, along with a pair of dark shades over her eyes for precaution. Zeke and four others—including the young Hunter that she'd yet to get the name of, and Boss—climbed into the front one with her. The others occupied the one in back. The cuffs burned her wrists and she shifted her hands uncomfortably.

"He's had some assistance recently. That's all I can tell you. You'll find out soon enough," Zeke replied.

"I sure am thirsty. I would advise humans to keep a safe distance away." She turned to him with a threatening smile, revealing her extended fangs. One of the Hunters on her other side pushed away from her as far as he could. She almost laughed out loud. Zeke seemed unfazed by her.

"I'm not stupid, either, Zeke. You're not human."

Everyone went still in the vehicle and stared at the two of them in silence. In a flash, his gun went off and he'd shot two of the humans, setting a ringing in her ears. She looked around frantically to see Boss unharmed. Only two unnamed Hunters had been killed, one that had sat in the front passenger seat, and the one on the other side of her. The young man that had been captive at The Compound had a look of fright, his knuckles white and gripping the seat in front of her. The driver had shifted briefly during the shock, but now acted nonchalant and oblivious.

Zeke turned to her. His mask was down and the helmet was off.

"I think it's best you just don't speak the rest of the trip."

Her nod was slow; her eyes wide. She didn't have to see anything to know for sure, she just did. Maybe it was instinct. Zeke was a Warrior. Not Exiled like Seth and his brothers. He worked for the Masters. If she was really being taken to the President, then that could only mean the world was in worse condition than they all thought.

The trip was long. They drove for hours. A flight was out of the question for her. But she knew they wouldn't waste days to get there. Her questions were answered as soon as dusk descended and her body could handle being outside long enough to be forced onto a train. Since the changes, the nation's capital had been mostly destroyed. People no longer resided there with the exception of the President in the White

House—and it was only him. There were no longer any Senate or House of Representatives or Congress. He made all of the laws now, and whatever he decided, it was final.

The train took them to Alexandria, Virginia and from there, they got back in similar sport utility vehicles again to take her to the capital. She slept most of the time. The exhaustion and the silver from the cuffs had got to be too much.

"Wake up."

She felt Zeke poke her in the rib.

When she sat up and looked around, she'd found they'd parked. They were there. Guards surrounded the vehicle with weapons.

"We're going to sit here for a while, until dusk, so that you can be escorted inside," he added. She shuddered and continued staring out the darkly tinted windows. It was hard to believe that almost two days had already passed since she'd left the safety of The Compound. She secretly hoped that Draven had found the video and that everything was going okay there with everyone. She definitely didn't want another rescue mission like with the Nathanial situation. It would be suicide for them. No. This time she was handling things on her own.

During their travels, Boss and the other Hunter had been moved to the other vehicle after another two humans were executed behind the train station. It was just her and Zeke alone in the SUV, with a driver of course, and she kept glancing at him from the corner of her eye. He had a familiar look to him. His hair was short and black, neatly trimmed, and he was tall and lean. His face was round, with wide bright green eyes--unlike the normal gold eyes seen in the other Fallen she knew.

"I don't know why I feel like I've seen you before," she said at last, daring to speak for the first time since he told her not to.

He turned to her with a frustrated sigh.

"I told you not to talk."

She shrugged and stared down at her hands. Her wrists had burn marks from the cuffs. Blood oozed from the wounds. She ignored the pain.

The guards outside tapped on the window to grab their attention. Zeke tugged on her shoulder. Night had started to set, making it safe to transport her from the vehicle to inside. Her mostly-dead heart thudded hard once in nervousness as she stepped into the building and allowed them to surround her. They escorted her toward the office.

Zarah was still barefoot and clothed in her pajamas from two nights ago. She felt icky. The thirst gnawed at her stomach, cramping it. Her legs were weak. She smelled a mix of human and Fallen through the halls.

"So nice of you to join us, Zarah," a voice said from the desk when they shoved her inside. She looked around to see that guards remained outside the office with the exception of her main escort, Zeke, and she was forced to stand in the center of the room.

She looked to the source of the voice to see the man she'd come to loathe—the man who wanted to end vampires—smiling at her from the desk. Beside him stood another man. She swallowed hard. He looked like a perfect blend of Seth and Draven. His hair was long with a mixture of dark auburn—almost a match to her hair color—and light brown hair. His eyes were a swirl of amber and navy. And he was so tall, she had to crane her neck. Fear spiked in her chest. It couldn't be. She blinked hard as she tried to will away a possible nightmare, only to find the images around her still there.

"I've heard a lot about you. Maybe you know my associate?" President Perkins added, motioning to the man that Zarah couldn't keep her eyes from.

"Do you know what he is?" she asked the president with caution. Her legs trembled and she started to fall. Zeke reached out and pulled her back up.

"Of course. And he's been a great help in hunting down you vile monsters. Your special little group though, I'm not so sure what to do about just yet. So we're going to wait and see."

The Fallen stepped around the desk and stared down at her with an amused smirk.

"So, how are my sons doing?"

Acknowledgements

As always, I thank all of my biggest supporters, family and friends, because without you I would've given up long ago. Thank you for continuing to read *The Guardians of the Night* trilogy, and I hope that you continue to read other future releases as well.

Also a big, huge many thanks to the wonderful book bloggers out there. Without you all, authors like me wouldn't be here. You rock!

About the Author

Pixie Lynn Whitfield resides in Texas with her husband, three stepchildren, cat and dog. When she's not writing, she's reading and blogging. *The Guardians of the Night* trilogy is her first published work, though there are plans for others to come in the near future. You can find her on Twitter or through Goodreads.

...